THE PEAKS OF SAN JACINTO

When hard man Roop Calmont rode into Pine Notch, folk predicted life in the town would never be the same again. Roop had come to help his rancher brother, Clayton, who was wrongly accused of rustling. A search for the real rustler leads Roop and Nancy, his brother's wife, to the San Jacinto hills, the domain of bandit leader El Toro. Finding the rustler isn't difficult, but bringing him out of the hills proves to be a grim adventure.

Books by Terry Murphy
in the Linford Western Library:

HE RODE WITH QUANTRILL
CANYON OF CROOKED SHADOWS
SAN CARLOS HORSE SOLDIER
MIDNIGHT LYNCHING
THE HUNTING MAN

TERRY MURPHY

THE PEAKS OF SAN JACINTO

Complete and Unabridged

LINFORD
Leicester

First published in Great Britain in 1999 by
Robert Hale Limited
London

First Linford Edition
published 2000
by arrangement with
Robert Hale Limited
London

British Library CIP Data

Murphy, Terry, *1962* –
    The peaks of San Jacinto.—Large print ed.—
Linford western library
1. Western stories
2. Large type books
I. Title
823.9'14 [F]

ISBN 0–7089–5633–5

Published by
F. A. Thorpe (Publishing) Ltd.
Anstey, Leicestershire

Set by Words & Graphics Ltd.
Anstey, Leicestershire
Printed and bound in Great Britain by
T. J. International Ltd., Padstow, Cornwall

This book is printed on acid-free paper

1

It was said that a wound to the head when fighting for the Confederacy had turned Roop Calmont into a cold-eyed killer. Whether or not this story was true didn't matter a damn to the folk of Pine Notch when he rode into their town one fine morning. It wasn't the cause but the effect that was worrying them. Roop had the kind of reputation in New Mexico that promised all hell would break loose wherever he happened to be.

Those who first saw him ride up were in Bennie Cault's general store. There were four of them: Bennie himself, old Matt Brown who helped out around the place, Ellie Brookes, the Pine Notch schoolma'am, and Carey Phillips, the lad who ran errands for the Star Ranch.

Cault was one of those greedy

1

businessmen who live in dread of a cold snap, wet spell, or a drought leading to a demand for goods he was out of. Consequently there was always more stock than the store was large enough to hold. The only two windows in the place, both facing out on West Street, had long been blinded by stacks of unopened boxes. No one in the place would have seen Calmont arrive if the door hadn't been left wide open because it was one of those mornings when even the breeze was too hot.

Bennie Cault stood motionless as he stared out through the doorway, the dried legumes he'd been bagging for Ellie forgotten. Calmont had that natural way in the saddle that defied anyone to tell where the rider ended and the horse began. Such a bond had been formed between man and animal that they had ceased to be separate entities. Calmont moved his head neither to left nor right, yet you could tell he was aware of everything around him. Ellie Brookes was kind of flustered in that secretly excited way even chaste women have when there's a dangerous man around. Carey, who had the long face of a hound dog and the poking-out teeth of a gopher, stood in reverent awe as the gunfighter smoothly dismounted. Old Matt made Ellie's face go red as a Texas sunset by muttering that he'd prefer to get the French pox from a saloon strumpet than a howdy from the likes of Roop Calmont.

'This is bad, this is bad,' Bennie said, voice quavering, his fat-fingered hands nervously clenching and unclenching, 'This town was ready to do what it could for Clay Calmont, but it sure isn't going to side with the likes of Roop.'

It was plain to all of them why Roop Calmont was here. His brother, Clayton Calmont, as likeable and peaceable a fellow as Roop was unsociable and downright dangerous, was in the town jail awaiting the visit of a judge due next week. Clayton had bought the Double J ranch that was tucked in close to the foot of the San Jacinto hills. That was a bit over a year ago when he and Nancy, his redheaded wife, had taken over the thriving outfit. Nancy was a striking woman, despite a slight turn in her right eye that you didn't notice until she tried to look straight at you. Mitch Bailey, the roughneck drifter Clayton had bought the spread from, hadn't been liked. That was probably why the Pine Notch folk had immediately taken a liking to the Calmonts.

Everything had been going real well, with Clayton talking of adding to the 3,000 head of beef on his spread, when he'd been arrested on a charge of rustling. This wasn't anything to do with the here and now, but was said to have taken place up in the Texas Panhandle before Clayton and Nancy moved to Pine Notch.

Most folk were of the opinion that the law, in the wiry shape of the taciturn, Deputy Marshal Orland Falk, a mysterious sort of man, had made a blunder. There was no way that the

4

gentle, kindly Clay Calmont would have done wrong. What was more, the refined Nancy Calmont wouldn't have tolerated a wrongdoer for a single moment. As far as Pine Notch was concerned, Clay Calmont was a solid citizen and an expert cattleman.

'You're too easy skeer'd, Bennie,' old Matt scathingly observed, moderating his criticism so as not to risk the job he had sweeping around the store and shifting boxes, barrels and the like. 'We've all heard what an all-fired good shootist Roop Calmont be, but that fella Falk who threw brother Clay in the jail is a deputy marshal. He ain't some boy pretender like Sheriff Decker. He's a Federal — '

'Maybe so, maybe so, Matt,' Bennie Cault conceded, 'but Falk's ridden out. All that stands between this town and the kind of mayhem Roop Calmont's likely to cause is Derek Decker, who ain't no more'n a kid only capable of using the toe of his boot to shift the town drunk off the sidewalk.'

'There's his deputy, Pat.' Carey Phillips praised one of his heroes while staring with worshipping eyes at the newcomer outside.

'Pat Shephard,' Matt Brown muttered a criticism. 'That sidewinder might be able to do something if Roop turns his back on him for long enough.'

An indignant Carey was about to defend the deputy, but instead he hissed in an urgent whisper, 'He's a-coming this way.'

Carey Phillips was doing a kind of childish bouncing up and down in his excitement, his front teeth more prominent than ever. The boy's mental age was never likely to catch up with his physical years. A few local folk treated him with sympathy, while the majority of them took advantage of the lad. Carey's boss, Will Bramley, exploited him.

Until Roop Calmont had turned up, Carey had been ready to leave with the shotgun Bramley had sent him into town to buy. The Star Ranch was plagued by jack-rabbits, and the owner had decided to blast the vermin off his land. Slackjawed, the boy now put the heavy firearm on the counter to stand with the others who were silently and apprehensively watching Roop Calmont's approach through sunlight still young enough to be hazy.

The gunman's walk was lithe, with none of the stiffness expected of a man who had been long in the saddle. Treading lightly, his booted feet didn't disturb dust too lazy to stir itself in the heat. He wasn't a big man; at a rough guess he stood no more than five feet nine inches tall. But there was something about him, an invisible force was perhaps the best description, that made him appear to be much larger. It would have been foolish to believe everything you heard about Roop Calmont, but enough of it was true to make even real hard men turn cautious.

Bennie Cault guessed the *Santa Fe New Mexican* had Roop about right with the story of how two young toughs had tried to boost their reputations by gunning him down in a Santa Fe hotel. Calmont had been sat at his dinner, and the newspaper had reported: *He shot one of his attackers in the right eye, the other through the heart, then went right on eating his meal. Rupert Calmont may well be immortal, and it would be suicidal to try to prove otherwise.*

That last sentence had to be exaggeration, yet the sight of Roop made it right easy to take up a belief in the supernatural. As he came in through the door the four people inside the store unconsciously moved closer together. They were put off balance by him. The way he kind of deliberately underplayed his entrance increased the power of his presence.

Pausing for a moment, his eyes flicked fast from left to right, checking for any threat the shadows inside the store might possibly hold. He was imprinting the surroundings on his mind in the manner of those who must rely on their instincts, and who live or die by the gun. He took off his stetson and bent in a stiff little courteous bow to Ellie Brookes. He was more handsome than any of the actors the four local folk had seen travelling with the company that had staged *Camille* in the town's New Theatre. Either his long, wavy fair hair concealed the scar, or the tale of the Civil War injury was false.

He bore no resemblance to his dark-haired, kind-eyed brother, Claymont. The story went that the two brothers were from a real respectable Tennessee family, which gave credence to yet another tale about Roop. This was that he was the bastard child of a group of itinerant ruffians who had, when passing the Calmont home years ago, taken the real baby Rupert from his cradle and left this one in his place.

Studying each of the three men present in turn, his steady, blue-eyed gaze making them anxious, Calmont selected the store owner.

'I'm looking for the sheriff's office,'

he said, making it a question rather than a statement.

Low but without the rough edge a whisper has, the gunfighter's voice had a peculiar quality. Disconcertingly, it didn't seem to issue directly from Calmont. His words were detached from him, sounding as if they came from beside where he stood. Without seeing his lips move you'd doubt that it was he who had spoken. It caused Bennie Cault and the others to look curiously to each side of Calmont as they listened to what he said.

'I works down there when I ain't here in the store,' old Matt announced proudly. 'I ain't hankering for a badge or nothing, not by a jugful. I'm just the jail-keep, but I does a good job.'

It seemed that Roop Calmont hadn't heard the old man. He stood in a relaxed kind of way that wouldn't fool a coot, his eyes staying on Bennie Cault.

Unnerved, Cault gulped as he struggled to put an answer together under Calmont's penetrating stare. At

10

his side, Carey Phillips's excitement was causing him to tremble. To the boy's way of thinking the infamous were much more inspiring and superior to the famous. There was a look of fanatical adoration on his face as he gazed at the newcomer.

'Head straight down West Street,' Bennie at last managed to reply, stretching out a fleshy arm to point-lessly indicate the direction that the walls of his store shut off from view. 'There's a turning dead opposite Riley's saloon. Go down theres a way and you'll see Sheriff Decker's place on your left. He's got your bro — '

Realizing his mistake, Bennie snapped off the end of his sentence, but it was too late. Calmont put together in his mind the rest of what Cault had been about to say.

'So, you know who I am,' Roop Calmont said, with a small smile that didn't reveal whether he resented or was pleased at having been recognized.

Bennie Cault began to shake from

11

fear as much as young Carey Phillips was from excitement. Perspiration beaded his brow and he had to ease his shirt away from a chubby body that had become sticky with sweat. Matt Brown lessened the strain for himself by biting off a lump of tobacco and chawing it with the few teeth he had left.

'We all thought that we knew . . . ' a fearful Ellie Brookes came in swiftly in the hope of taking Calmont's attention from Bennie.

Raising a surprisingly small, slim hand to stop her talking, the gunfighter gave Ellie a charmingly warm smile. 'You don't owe me no explanation, ma'am.'

Ellie, who was pushing forty, reacted like one of the girls in her school. Blushing prettily, something she could do well because she was a handsome woman, she did an involuntary half curtsy. A good-looking woman can sure make a fool of a man, but that don't amount to much compared to the real daft way some men can get an otherwise sensible woman to act. But the chivalrous Roop Calmont saw the quaint rather than the ridiculous side of her behaviour. He acknowledged Ellie's impromptu genuflection with a sweeping bow. Straightening up, he continued to hold his stetson as his face went serious when he asked another question of Cault.

'This Decker, the sheriff, what kind of a man is he?'

Bennie shook his head. 'Shucks, he isn't a man. Derek Decker's naught but a boy.'

'No town should ask a boy to do a man's job,' Roop Calmont declared, his voice quieter than ever.

Cault had a ready answer, but not one he was prepared to give to Calmont. The town council, of which he was a member, had got the boy on the cheap. Decker had come into town after hitching a ride on the stage. No more than eighteen, he'd had a pair of high-heeled cowboy boots that were too new on his feet, and an expression that was too old for his years on his face. That night Decker had sampled everything liquid in Riley's place, and had lost every cent he had playing double 'O'. Two things had happened the following morning. One was that Claude Sheen, who owned Pine Notch's Peak View Hotel, somehow learned that the kid was Senator Decker's wayward son, and the other that the boy was looking for work.

The town had needed a sheriff. Pat Shephard would have been ideal if it weren't for his past as a desperado. Pine Notch had voted Decker into the job, and had made Shephard his deputy. That way the council had two for the price of one, with Decker doing the swaggering and Shephard doing the fighting.

'Decker said he could do the job,' Cault replied defensively.

'The difference between saying and doing is the same as that between living and dying.' Calmont indulged in some homespun philosophy, speaking to himself before he looked at Cault to say, 'I'm obliged to you for your help, sir.'

He extended more Southern courtesy toward Ellie with yet another bow, before turning to make his silent-tread way to the door.

Though her face was still pink from her exchanges with the handsome gunslinger, Ellie was as relieved as the others to be free of the nerve-tightening tension his presence created. Carey Phillips, overwhelmed by having been so close to a real hero, was eager to get back to the Star Ranch to tell that he had actually met Roop Calmont. Keeping adoring eyes on the departing Calmont, he reached blindly behind him for the shotgun. When his groping fingers located the stock, Carey accidentally knocked the barrel of the gun against an iron kettle that stood on the counter. The impact made a metallic clunk.

At the door, Calmont was galvanized

by the sound. Dropping to a crouch as he spun round, his hand slapped the leather of his gun holster.

Ellie screamed, a terrified Carey Phillips cowered down in front of the counter, eyes bulging and his thin legs tangling awkwardly. The instinct of self-preservation lent Bennie Cault an agility that denied his bulk as he put a distance between himself and the quaking boy.

It was Matt Brown who saved the moment. His body misshapen by the twisted joints of oldsters who have spent too much of their lives outdoors, he stepped bravely in front of Carey. The boy couldn't stop cringing, even though it was now the old man and not himself who was looking into the muzzle of Calmont's .45.

With a resolute expression doubling the wrinkles of his face, Matt Brown spoke firmly to Roop Calmont. 'You're almighty jumpy, mister. The boy was just reaching for a scattergun his boss sent him into town to buy. The

16

dang-blamed thing ain't even loaded, yet you're ready to shoot the lad dead, have him as cold as a wagon tyre. It's plain 'nuff the lad ain't exactly smart as a steel trap.'

Easing his body slowly upright, Roop Calmont took his hand away from his gun as he apologized quietly to Carey Phillips. 'My mistake, son.'

With that he lifted his stetson an inch or two to Ellie Brookes, turned once more, and walked out of the store.

Cault, Ellie, and Carey, who was standing on shaking legs now, clutched at the counter as if fearing they would be drawn into the vacuum of fear left behind by Roop Calmont. Old Matt bit off another chaw of tobacco in an attempt to appear unmoved and nonchalant, although he was obviously shaking from the incident with the gunslinger.

'You stay right still until he's mounted up and ridden away, young Carey,' Bennie Cault warned earnestly. 'Don't you go waking no more snakes. I don't want this place of mine shot full of holes. There's no profit in barrels of pickles and crackers filled with lead.'

Still too traumatized to speak, Carey then managed to blurt out, 'I'm right sorry, Mr Cault.' He looked admiringly at Matt Brown, who, minutes earlier would have been an unlikely idol for the boy. 'That took real guts, facing up to Roop Calmont like you did, Mr Brown.'

'That weren't nothing, son,' Matt Brown said, preening himself, pleased by Carey's admiration. 'There weren't no real danger from that fella. Maybe he's a gunslinger now, but afore that he was a greyback, a disciplined Confederate soldier. I knows these things, boy, 'cos I fought at Cold Harbour. His sort knows right from wrong. No, sirree, we weren't in no danger from him, but I could tell you tales of the old days that would make the hair on that thick head o' yourn stand on end. I bin up in them hills on nights so dark that even the bats stayed at home.'

'We know those tales off by heart because we've heard them so often, Matt,' Bennie Cault protested.

'I ain't never heard them, Mr Cault,' Carey Phillips sulkily complained.

'And you're not going to hear them now,' Cault snapped. 'This here's a store not a dram shop for standing around jawing in all day long.'

The store proprietor relaxed now that nothing remained of Roop Calmont other than the slow thud of his horse's hoofs on the dusty road. Bending, he scooped dried legumes out of a bushel basket for Ellie Brookes, who, with a wistful softness in her eyes, gazed at the spot where she had last seen Roop Calmont standing.

'I can't believe those two men are brothers,' she mused. 'Mr Clayton Calmont has strongly supported the school since he has lived here. He is so quiet and respectable.'

'Maybe they're not brothers,' Cault mumbled as he juggled weights on a set of brass scales. 'Maybe that tale is true.'

'Whatever tale is that, Mr Cault?' Ellie asked, curiosity animating her. It was evident it would take her an awful long time, maybe forever, to get over having met Roop Calmont. His type either scared men or had them reaching for their guns, but what they did to women was a mystery.

'I shouldn't have spoken. It's not a tale for ladies,' an uncomfortable Bennie Cault answered.

'Oh dear,' Ellie said, a bit miffed. 'But I've never for one moment believed that Mr Clayton Calmont has done anything to be put in jail for. He will be so relieved to have his brother here. I expect they'll get together to put things right.'

'Huh,' Matt Brown gave a snort of disgust. 'Roop and Clay Calmont get together! You cain't hitch a horse with a coyote, Miss Ellie.'

'I'm afraid that I don't quite follow you, Mr Crown.'

'Them two brothers are as unalike as chalk and cheese,' old Matt grunted.

'But they are brothers,' Ellie Brookes insisted.

'I don't think Clayton Calmont will feel the same about that as you do, Miss Ellie,' Cault said, squeezing the top of her bag of legumes shut.

'Are you saying, Mr Cault, that Clayton Calmont won't welcome his brother's help?'

'Help!' Matt gave another of his snorts. 'That Roop will make things a thousand times worse for Clay. I know for sure that boy's innocent, and it would be only a matter of time till it was proved. But Clay'll be finished if Roop makes any kind of a move to help him. Mark my words. If Roop Calmont takes a hand in this, then gunsmoke will rise as high as the San Jacinto Peaks.'

Picking up the shotgun to put it in Carey Phillips's hands, Cault manually moved the gaping-mouthed boy towards the door, speaking to Ellie and Matt over his shoulder.

'The only good thing about Roop riding in is that Nancy Calmont won't be left all alone out there on the Double J.'

'I wouldn't be so bold as to judge the Mr Calmont who has just left here,' Ellie said slowly and with a little shiver, like she was all caught up with a mixture of envy and fear, 'but I just can't imagine Nancy permitting a man such as that to enter her house. Surely she wouldn't be safe?'

'I guess what I said about Roop led you wrong, Miss Ellie,' Matt Brown did his best to explain. 'A pretty girl like Nancy right out there, with the San Jacinto hills alive with border ruffians, couldn't ask for a safer man to have in her house than Roop Calmont.'

Frowning, Ellie Brookes looked from old Matt to Bennie Cault. Though always a bit indecisive around men, she was ever self-possessed and certain of her own judgements. Either temporarily or permanently, Roop Calmont had robbed her of those character attributes. That was something Claude

Sheen, Pine Notch's bachelor hotelier, hadn't been able to do in the two years Ellie had been in town. His persistent but unsuccessful pursuit of the schoolma'am had Sheen, in Matt Brown's vernacular, 'catawamptitiously chawed up'.

'I do confess that you gentlemen have me all confused,' Ellie said in a way that invited them to tell her more about Roop Calmont.

'Nothing could be simpler than understanding Roop Calmont, Miss Ellie,' Bennie Cault assured her.

'That's sure true 'nuff', old Matt agreed. 'No town nor the folk in it have been the same when Roop's rode out as they were when Roop rode in.'

'Which is something all of us in Pine Notch have to worry about,' Bennie Cault said quietly and fearfully.

'If we ain't careful, Pine Notch could be exfluncticated,' Matt Brown added.

Neither Cault nor Brown could tell whether the schoolma'am was alarmed or aroused. They decided, silently and separately, that it was probably a mixture of both. Then they forgot her as the menace of Roop Calmont forced itself back into their fretting minds.

2

By standing on the edge of the cot in his cell and stretching his arms up to a painful extreme, Clayton Calmont could grasp the bars of the small window. Pulling himself up, he could hold on for a short while to take a look out. It wasn't much of a view, just the southern corner of the roof of Riley's saloon and a section of blue sky above. But it gave him some comfort. It was a tenuous but valuable link with the outside world. The drawback was that while it somehow made him feel closer to Nancy, it also filled him with anxiety. As an outdoor man, he felt frustration, too.

His wife was his major worry. Clayton would have been content to sweat it out in this cell which was unbearably hot during the day, confident that Orland Falk, a hard but reasonable man, would discover he had made a mistake. But, though he could not think of an alternative, Clayton was aware that he couldn't wait because Nancy was at risk. With the Double J herd impounded, they'd had to pay off their three loyal hands. They had been just ordinary cowpokes, not fast guns, but it usually discouraged drifters when they found men about a place. That had left Nancy all alone, and no more than a day or two would pass on the Double J without some saddletramp riding in.

Dropping down to stand on the stone floor, circling bent arms to ease the pain in them, Clayton Calmont sat on his bed and for the thousandth time tried to fathom how everything could have gone so wrong. If he found the answer to that question he would be in a position to put the whole loco matter to rights. The way things stood right then, Falk, the Federal deputy marshal, had Clayton, who on evidence was a cattle thief, and had no need to investigate further. It was now a matter for the judge, who wouldn't be arriving in Pine Notch until next week. If there was a case to answer, and on the face of it there definitely was, Clayton would doubtless be taken to Santa Fe to stand trial, further than ever away from his wife.

It had begun late one day with the arrival of a stranger at the Double J. Nancy and he had watched the rider's slow approach. He came from a direction that said he'd ridden along the foothills. There was nothing unusual in having a caller. Some were decent but restless men wanting to discover what lay behind the furthest hill. Others were the dregs of society, either fleeing from a crime already carried out, or heading toward an about-to-be committed felony.

Each time they turned off the trail to come to the ranch, singly, in pairs, or small groups, Clayton would weigh up their appearance before deciding to offer hospitality or issue an order to keep riding. Clayton knew that his dark, tough appearance helped. What the men he moved on didn't know was that he hadn't the heart of a fighting man. If necessary he would defend Nancy with his life, but the thought of violence for violence's sake appalled him.

Looking back, he guessed both he and Nancy had known from the start there was something different about this particular rider. Neither a saddle-tramp nor a renegade, the black-clad horseman obviously took a pride in his appearance. While he was still at a distance, the long, fair hair coming from under a stetson to almost shoulder length, had caused Clayton's heart to miss a beat. Just for a split second he feared it was his brother, Roop, riding up on them. Having only told Nancy that he had a brother, deliberately not going into any detail, he knew he would have a lot of hard explaining to do if this was the wild, two-fisted, fast-drawing Roop riding up on them.

Clayton had made an audible sigh of relief on realizing this wasn't his brother. The rider came on unhurried, walking his horse, with light from the westering sun causing the silver conchos studding his leather chaps to sparkle.

Coming in through the piñon-wood gate of their fence, he dismounted, taking off his stetson. With the last of the day's sun burnishing his long hair yellow, he beat the dust off the hat against his thigh. Studying Clayton, just long enough to gain some kind of impression without being rude, the stranger acknowledged Nancy's presence with a nod. Then he turned his attention to Clayton.

'Would you be Clayton Calmont?'

'That's me,' Clayton had readily admitted, 'and I've got two questions of my own; who's asking, and why?'

With a nod that acknowledged these were fair questions, the stranger replied. 'My name is Orland Falk. As to why I'm here, I'd like to explain that inside the house, if I wouldn't be imposing.'

'Please, come in,' Nancy, a good judge of people and apparently impressed by the stranger, had invited. 'Would you like some refreshment?'

'Coffee would cut the dust, ma'am, if it's not too much bother.'

He had followed them into the ranch house, his spur-chains chinking as he walked. Not as tall as Clayton, Falk didn't need to bend his head in the low, pine-ceilinged room. He stood looking appreciatively around him at the tidy room, good manners preventing him from taking a seat while Nancy stood making the coffee. He had then joined them at the table, making small talk instead of explaining his reason for calling on them.

'Does your place stretch right out to the foothills?' he had asked with real interest as Nancy sliced up a pie she had made for the next day.

'The Double J goes right to where you have to climb the San Jacinto hills to go further,' Clayton had proudly answered.

'You've got a nice ranch here, Calmont.'

'We've only got to the tune of about three thousand head of cattle,' Clayton had said, adding modestly, 'That's no more than homesteading, I reckon, but I've got plans for expanding, Falk.'

Giving another of his assenting nods, Falk had asked, 'Been here long?'

'Fourteen months,' Nancy had answered, always one to be precise with dates, time, money and the like.

'I don't want to appear inhospitable, but you ask a whole heap of questions, mister,' Clayton had complained at that time.

Not speaking for a while, Falk had said thanks with a smile as Nancy had gestured toward the cut pie, pushing his plate forward for another helping. Taking a sip of coffee, he looked steadily at Clayton over the rim of his raised mug.

'I owe it to you, Calmont,' he said, in a voice that was as even as his gaze, 'to tell you that I'm a range detective. It's

Deputy Marshal Falk.'

'Why would that bring you to me?'

Clayton had been putting two and two together in his head by then. It seemed likely that Falk might well have the right surname in Calmont, but the wrong first name. Brother Rupert, despite his way of life, had until then, as far as Clayton was aware, not seriously transgressed the law. Most probably that had changed.

'Seems like I've got to answer that with another question, Calmont,' Falk had said apologetically. 'You ever been up around the Panhandle?'

'Yep,' Clayton hadn't hesitated in replying. 'We moved down here from there after me and Nancy met and got wed. I was ramrod on the Bar Diamond for Major Steadman. Has something happened to the major?'

With a shake of his head, Falk had answered, 'Not that I've heard. Did you know the IJ Ranch up there?'

'Isuelt Jacob's spread?' Clayton had checked. 'Yep, of course. The IJ is the biggest outfit in the Panhandle. I guess everybody knows of the place.'

Clayton had probably noticed then but hadn't realized the significance of it until later, that Falk had moved a little as he sat at the table. He'd shifted his hips so that the butt of his holstered gun was accessible before he had cautiously asked his next question.

'I've got to ask this, Calmont, and I don't want you to go off sort of half-cocked.'

'I'm a peaceable man, Falk. Anyhow, I'm not likely to make some kind of play with Nancy sitting here,' Clayton had answered, and he could feel again now his apprehension at that time.

Shadows were crowding the room as the sun set. Nancy had broken the tension by standing to light the oil lamp and place it on the table. In the half-light, Falk's face, which was as dark as that of an Indian and contrasted sharply with his light-coloured hair, had taken on an additional hardness that made it menacing.

'Your three thousand head, Calmont,' Falk had begun. 'You got a bill of sale?'

'Nope,' Clayton had replied easily. 'They came with the ranch when I bought it from Mitch Bailey.'

'But the Double J is your brand?'

'Yep, it was already registered to Bailey, and I took it on.'

'Who did your branding?' Falk had enquired sharply.

'Mitch Bailey, I guess.'

'The thing is, I took a look at the brand on my way in,' Falk said, leaning over the table to write invisibly with a forefinger, 'and an IJ, like this, is easily altered to JJ, the Double J. Whoever changed the brand did a mighty clever job, but it won't stand close inspection. Those beef out there on your land, Calmont, were rustled from the IJ outfit up in the Panhandle.'

Nancy's shock had silently linked up with his, and the two of them were dumbstruck. At the time Clayton had purchased the Double J from Bailey he had considered him to be a rough

34

diamond. Since then, from talk around Pine Notch, he'd first learned that Mitch Bailey was a reformed desperado. But it later was general news that Bailey was back on the outlaw trail. Now all the signs were that Bailey had owned the Double J just long enough to change the brand on cattle he had rustled, and sell the outfit to Clayton.

'I'm telling you now, Falk,' Clayton had been forceful under threat, 'that I wouldn't homestead with a rustled herd. I paid cash to Bailey for the Double J, and Nancy was with me at the time and saw the money change hands.'

'I don't doubt your word, Calmont.'

'Then it's Bailey that you want,' Nancy had blurted hopefully.

'I'm afraid it doesn't work like that, ma'am,' Falk had told her with what was plainly genuine regret. 'You see, all the evidence I have is against your husband, and it's enough for him to stand trial. That means I'm duty bound to take him in and let a judge do the deciding.'

'That just isn't fair. My husband isn't guilty of anything,' Nancy had protested. Her mass of red hair had somehow become disarrayed in sympathy with her fighting spirit.

'Then he'll need to prove that to the court, ma'am.'

'How?' Nancy challenged the detective despairingly.

'I know that I'll strike you as being callous, ma'am,' an uncomfortable Falk apologized in advance, 'but that is not up to me.'

'I understand that,' Clayton had said, slipping an arm round his wife. 'What happens now?'

'I'll have to take you in and hand you over in the custody of the sheriff in Pine Notch.'

'What about my wife?'

'Is there an hotel in Pine Notch?' Orland Falk put a suggestion into his question.

'Yes, there's Claude Sheen's — '

36

'No,' Nancy interrupted her husband. 'This is our place, Clayton, and I intend to stay here until you come back. You won't be away for long, I'm sure of that.'

Clayton was unhappy at his wife staying out there on her lonesome. Falk was about to attempt to persuade her, but an obvious change of mind made him thank her for the coffee and pie. Standing up from the table then, Falk had made it plain that he expected Clayton to get ready to leave.

All of this had been unexpected, ridiculous, and unfair, but there had been nothing Clayton could have done about it. Trying to assure Nancy that it would all work out, he had allowed Falk to take him into Pine Notch and hand him into the custody of Sheriff Derek Decker. Clayton's hope that he could make an arrangement with the local sheriff that would allow him to go home was quashed by Falk's insistence that

Decker keep him under lock and key.

He heard voices out in the office now. One of them would be the constantly morose Pat Shephard. It was too early for old Matt Brown to be taking over for the night. Though the old-timer couldn't take the worry over Nancy away, he made imprisonment tolerable for Clayton by telling stories, many of them too tall to be credible, of days long gone, or playing cards with Clayton through the bars of his cell.

Two lots of footsteps were coming down the passageway. Clayton heard Pat Shephard say grumblingly, 'I'm not opening up. I'll give you five minutes to talk to him, but you stay outside.'

'That's fine with me.'

For a moment Clayton either couldn't recognize that voice, or he didn't want to. But the footsteps kept on coming and he knew that he had to face the unwelcome truth: his brother Roop was paying him a visit.

★ ★ ★

38

'What can I do for you, mister?' Derek Decker looked up from where he sat to calmly enquire, though he was far from calm on the inside.

Word had reached him earlier that Roop Calmont had come to town and was visiting his brother at the jailhouse. Now the infamous gunman had made his approach in Riley's saloon, just as Decker had planned it. He wanted people around when he met a man with Calmont's reputation. Up to now being the sheriff of Pine Notch had been the best time of his life. He had gained a respect of sorts, and even his father had stopped hounding him in case he should bring further disgrace on the family name. Having once practised so as to at least grasp the rudiments of a fast draw, he had set out to improve his speed since the Pine Notch council had pinned the silver star on his chest. But now, for the first time since becoming sheriff, he faced the stark realization that he was acting out a charade. The gunbelt hanging on his narrow hips meant danger rather than protection in the presence of Roop Calmont.

'Don't ask a question to which you already have the answer, kid.' Decker found Calmont's strange voice to be additionally unnerving. The gunman's eyes penetrated his, seemingly going right through into his head and finding the self-doubts and uncertainty there. He glanced quickly round the saloon for a reassuring sighting of his deputy. Shephard, a hard man and a fast gun, might or might not be a match for Roop Calmont, but at least he would come a lot closer than Decker did. But Pat Shephard wasn't there. It wasn't yet time for old Matt Brown to take over duty guarding the jail.

'You give me the answer, Calmont,' Decker said, pleased with how confident he had sounded when speaking the words. He lifted the bottle on the table in front of him, signalling to the barkeep to bring a second glass. 'Will you take a drink with me?'

'I don't drink, kid.'

The second use of 'kid' caused Decker to flinch. Calmont had a way of making it sound real insulting. Now the gunman was pointing at him, and explaining why. 'Right now you're looking at a finger, kid, but if we don't agree on a certain matter, then it's my .45 that you'll be staring at, savvy?'

'This certain matter is your brother?' Decker asked, reasoning that talking was a whole lot better than shooting, especially when you're bound to be on the losing side.

'You've got it right. Tonight I'm riding out to check the Double J over. But I'll be back in the morning, kid, and next time I ride out to the ranch, Clayton will be riding at my side.'

'That won't be possible,' Derek Decker said, fervently wishing that he was older, stronger, faster, braver. 'A Federal deputy marshal gave me orders to keep Clayton Calmont locked up.'

Leaning just slightly forward, no more than an inch or two, Calmont caused Decker to cringe. 'There's no

Federal deputy marshal in town now, kid, so I'm giving the orders: I'll collect my brother soon after first light in the morning.'

The way Roop Calmont had spoken left no room for discussion or negotiation, most certainly not refusal. Picking up the bottle in his right hand, Decker wasn't sure whether he had done so to refill his glass, or to show Calmont that his gun hand was occupied.

'I can't let you take your brother from the jail.'

'You've got it wrong, kid,' Calmont told him with a ghost of a smile. 'You just can't stop me from freeing Clayton.'

'Perhaps he can, perhaps he can't,' a voice said from behind Roop Calmont, slightly to his left. 'But I can, and right now I'm behind you, and I've got you covered.'

'I know where you are and what you're up to, Shephard,' Calmont said. 'I had you placed the moment you stepped in the door.'

It worried Decker that Pat Shephard was shaken by what Roop Calmont had said, but he felt better when he saw his deputy return to his customary self-assured style.

'That don't make no difference, Calmont,' Shephard said. 'What I want you to do right now is unbuckle your gunbelt, pass it to Sheriff Decker, than turn around real careful and I'll take you back over to share the jailhouse with your brother.'

'I've got a notion to oblige you, Shephard. The only problem is — '

Decker was so absorbed with what Calmont was saying that he was unprepared for the gunman's sudden burst of action. Swinging his left hand back hard and with astonishing accuracy, he caught Shephard a lip-mashing, backhanded blow in the mouth. It sent the deputy flying backwards, knocking over a table and crashing to the floor, without a chance to pull the trigger of the gun he was holding. At the same time, Roop

Calmont drew his .45 and fired. The bottle Decker was holding exploded. Glass was blown across his hand, cutting it open, and then what felt to be a thousand shards of glass were slashing his face to pieces.

Bleeding profusely from face and hand, Decker sank back in his chair. He watched Calmont spin on one heel and lash out with his right foot to kick the six-shooter out of Shephard's hand.

Spinning over and over in the air, the deputy's gun hit the walnut panelling that came part way up the wall of the saloon. A confident Roop Calmont was walking to the door, not looking back to see what was going on behind him. When he was at the door, passing Billy Riley, the proprietor of the saloon, who seemed about to say something to him, but decided against the idea, Calmont kept going as Pat Shephard shouted:

'You're a dead man, Calmont.' The deputy's mouth sprayed blood as he cried out.

Roop Calmont went out of the saloon without once looking back.

* * *

As the shadows lengthened outside of the ranch house, so did a sense of dread develop alarmingly in Nancy Calmont. Fear was bringing her close to fainting. The three ruffians had arrived at a little after noon that day, and she had been trying to get rid of them since. But now, after fetching bottles of rye whiskey from their saddle-bags, they had obviously decided to stay the night. They were becoming progressively drunker as they constantly swigged from the bottles.

One was a Mexican, squat, fat and greasyfaced, whom the other two referred to as 'Snake'. He laughed a lot when there was nothing to laugh at, but Nancy recognized that if there was any real humour in him, it in no way lessened the threat that he was to her. The second man, whose name Nancy had gathered was Mark Butterfield, was middle-aged, unwashed and unshaven, with a similar mental instability to the Mexican. The third man, tall and thin, the doleful expression on his face accentuated by a drooping moustache, was apparently the leader. He put out a hand to grab Nancy by the wrist as she was reaching for the oil lamp.

'What you thinking of doing, Red?' he asked with a smile that jiggled his heavy moustache but didn't get up as high as his eyes.

'It's getting dark,' Nancy quaveringly replied. 'I'm going to light the lamp.'

He shook his head. 'We don't need no light.' Reaching out, he held her chin between the thumb and forefinger of his right hand, moving her head a little to study her profile. 'Weren't you once a Santa Fe saloon girl?'

Indignation and anger temporarily overcoming her fear, Nancy jerked away from him. 'How dare you? You'll soon be sorry. I'm expecting my husband home at any moment.'

The man threw back his head and laughed. The Mexican laughed with him, longer and louder, and Butterfield dutifully joined in.

'Now a pretty woman like you didn't ought a lie, Red,' the man with the moustache chided her as if she were an infant. 'I hear tell, and I don't doubt that it's true, that your man's been tossed into the calaboose down in Pine Notch.'

Going cold all over, Nancy was momentarily paralysed by the frightful realization that this border ruffian knew that Clayton wouldn't be coming home. That she was all alone out here.

'Allow me to introduce myself,' he was saying. 'Sergeant John G. Wheeler, Company C of the 14th Pennsylvania Cavalry. I earned my medal for 'Gallantry in Action' at Stone River, Tennessee.'

'Why should I want to know who you are?' Nancy asked contemptuously.

His arm went round her waist, Nancy struggled to get away but he was too strong. She kicked him hard in the shin, causing her own toes agony. It only made Wheeler laugh, and the Mexican laughed with him. Butterfield joined in the laughter once again. It was a crazy discordant sound that rose to a crescendo, echoing round the room, bouncing about inside of Nancy's head until she feared for her sanity. A heavy moustache came ticklingly against her cheek and Wheeler's long fingers eagerly began to tear at her clothing.

★   ★   ★

Roop Calmont mounted up outside the saloon as a spectacular sunset was making way for a welcome coolness that readied Pine Notch for the coming of night. Though the meeting with his brother, the first for many years, had been stiff and awkward in the beginning, Clayton had eventually agreed that he needed help. Worry over his wife, whom Roop had never met, was what finally convinced him. Yet, even so, Clayton had exacted a promise from Roop that any assistance he gave must be within the law and without gratuitous violence.

They both knew that Clayton's only salvation lay in tracking down Mitch Bailey and handing him over to the law. Roop had been prepared to do this alone, but Clayton insisted that he wanted to be part of it, despite the fact being broken out of jail would be another black mark against him.

Nancy's safety was Clayton's priority, and Roop was riding out to the Double J now. He had assured Clayton that he would call out on reaching the house, identifying himself and saying that Clayton had sent him. Although not seeking reward, Roop had been gratified by the immense relief exhibited by his brother on knowing that his wife was to be taken care of.

Wanting to reach the Double J at a reasonably early hour, he pushed his horse down the town's West Street at a steady pace. The buildings got sparser as he neared the end of town, the last small wooden structure having the look of a schoolroom. It was shaded by a row of giant cottonwoods, but he could make out a singlestorey annexe that had the look of living-quarters.

Standing on the porch, clothed in shadow but splendidly poised, was the figure of a woman. Something familiar about her had Roop rein in his roan horse.

'Why, it's Mr Calmont!'

The surprise in her voice was bogus. Recognizing Ellie Brookes, Roop was pretty sure that she had been watching him come down the street. Watching and waiting.

When he stopped beside the porch, pushing the stetson back on his head and looking down at her, the schoolteacher seemed strangely more ill at ease with herself than she was him. As a woman aware that she would be soon past her best, she was plainly forcing herself forward, completely out of character, searching for what she thought she had missed before it was too late. Frightened by her own forwardness, she was tensed like a doe ready for flight.

'It's a warm evening,' she remarked, raising a tumbler she had been drinking from. 'I find this apple cider refreshing. Would you care for a glass?'

The yellow-check dress that she wore flattered a figure that needed no help to look good. The 'V' at the neck showed skin that was golden-tanned. What attracted him to her most of all was that she was neither unconscious of her beauty nor cared a cuss about it.

Remaining in the saddle, Roop Calmont was undecided. There was some urgency in him going to his brother's ranch, although he was beginning to see an arrival at first light as less traumatic for Nancy Calmont.

Ellie had moved to the edge of the porch. The perfume from some night-scented flowers growing at the sides of the steps came to him. It was a deciding factor.

'That's a mighty kind invitation, Miss Ellie,' Roop Calmont said as he dismounted.

3

Aware that he was backlit by the dawn, Roop Calmont pulled his roan to a halt and surveyed the distant ranch house through cautious eyes. There were just two cow-horses penned out back. That ruled out anyone being there with Nancy, but he couldn't take a chance by riding in on her. Clayton hadn't had the chance to say what kind of woman his wife was, whether she could use a gun or not. More importantly, if she was likely to. One thing was certain: Roop would be nothing more than a stranger to her. He would have a problem explaining that he was Clayton's brother after she'd filled his belly full of lead with a Sharps rifle.

Roop heeled his horse into a walk, approaching the house slowly, ready to drop out of the saddle at the first sign of a ray of morning sunlight glinting off a gunbarrel. He had left Ellie sleeping in her bed. Asleep she looked very girlish and vulnerable, awake she had been the strangest, hot-blooded woman he had ever known, and he'd known quite a few. In a way she reminded him of men he had come across who'd reached middle age living mundane lives. One day, suddenly and without warning, they would avidly seek adventure with no regard to their own safety. They always struck him as being motivated by a death wish. Ellie Brookes didn't have a death wish, but what she suffered from had to be very similar.

He was struck by the cleanliness of the house. The paintwork looked new and the windows were bright. That figured. Brother Clayton liked everything neat and orderly, and he would have chosen a woman who was the same as himself in that way.

Yet the building appeared deserted and forlorn. Had it not been for the two dun-coloured horses in the corral, he would assume that Clayton's wife had left shortly after the deputy marshal had taken her husband off.

Dismounting at the side of the house, he moved carefully round to the front on foot, back tight against the wooden walls. Close beside the door, he thought it looked to be open. Drawing his .45, Roop lightly and quietly used the muzzle to prod the door. It swung inward easily on oiled hinges.

Stepping quickly inside, back-heeling the door so that it slammed against the wall, proving no one was concealed behind it, he quickly scanned the room. The only occupant was a woman sitting on a chair, her upper body slumped face down on the table. A mass of red hair was spread out on the rough surface. Roop hadn't asked Clayton the colour of his wife's hair, but guessed this had to be her.

Taking a step closer, he saw the bare arms stretched out across the table were bruised black and blue. What clothing she had on had been torn to shreds, and her face lay in a pool of dark-red blood.

★ ★ ★

'Miss Ellie don't answer the door, Mr Sheen,' reported the schoolboy to the hotelier who had sent him on an errand to the schoolhouse.

This was worrying news for the love-lorn Claude Sheen. Sheriff Derek Decker had Pine Notch on a state of alert that morning. It was a town divided, too, but not in any acrimonious sense. Just about everyone there was loyal to the law-abiding Clayton Calmont, but hostile to the wild and wayward Roop. If there was any way they could have got Clayton out of jail, most Pine Notch folk would have done so. At the same time they were totally opposed to their town and its laws being abused by his brother.

Roop Calmont had said, threatened really, that he would come into town that morning and get his brother out of

56

jail. Everyone in New Mexico knew that when Roop set his mind to something he always did it. Extra to that was the fact that whatever he was up to was always bad news. With no time to get word to the outlying ranchers, the sheriff had to make what use he could of the few men in town. Carey Phillips, who had been sent out by his boss to shoot rabbits, had brought the scatter-gun into Bennie Cault's store for more cartridges. Enlisted by Decker, Carey was now in the jailhouse, sitting in a chair outside of Clayton Calmont's cell, the shotgun lying across his skinny thighs, uncertain whether the responsibility of guarding Calmont made him feel good or scared the pants off him.

Pat Shephard, Decker's only real fighting man, was standing sentry beside the schoolhouse at the entry to town. Ida Cault, an overweight, lazy woman, had been forcibly recruited by her husband to mind the store. Satisfied that it would be a case of business as usual and he would lose no money,

Bennie Cault, armed with a .50 calibre buffalo gun that would blow Roop to pieces, if Bennie could both successfully aim it and withstand the recoil, paraded up and down in the road outside of the jail. Old Matt Brown had declared it would be a 'sin to Crockett' if he didn't use knowledge gained at the battle of Pea Ridge, the only engagement of the Civil War in which Red Indian troops formally participated.

'Because you won't see me, you may think I've absquatulated,' Matt explained to Decker, 'but I'll come sneakin' out of the shadows to cut up didoes soon's Roop shows up.'

Decker hadn't seen Matt since, but the oldtimer hadn't 'absquatulated' as Cault had spotted him sitting in an alleyway sharpening a Bowie knife. The chances of Matt getting close enough to use a knife on Roop Calmont were negligible.

The only other helper Decker had was a mailorder cowboy, a tenderfoot wearing all the proper clothes, who'd arrived on the stage the previous day. Paul Landers had come out West to gain material for a book he was writing. Eager for experience, but totally naive in the ways of the West, Landers had agreed to assist Decker. The chubby young Easterner was acting as a look-out, perched high and precariously in one of the huge cottonwoods on the edge of town.

As he was thinking that a lot of luck would be needed when Roop arrived, Decker saw Claude Sheen hurrying up to him. Openly admitting that with his out-of-condition body and genteel manner he would be more of a hindrance than a help in a fight, Claude had taken charge of organizing the people of the town. Having called at every house giving instructions that no child should be allowed to go to school, the hotelier wanted to be totally certain by ensuring that Ellie Brookes kept the schoolhouse doors locked. If Roop Calmont should take young hostages he would be able to hold the town to ransom and free his brother.

'You got a problem, Claude?' the sheriff enquired, eyeing the flat roof of Martha Gibbon's haberdashery store opposite as a place where he could lie in wait. He sure wasn't going to face Roop Calmont on the street.

'Couldn't rightly say,' an anguished Sheen replied. 'I sent Len Steward's boy down to the schoolhouse, but Miss Ellie didn't answer the door.'

'Could be she overslept, Claude.'

'That's not like Miss Ellie on a school day. I'm a bit worried, Sheriff, as that Roop Calmont is capable of anything.'

'Then you'd best go take a look,' Decker advised. 'Watch yourself, though. That's the end of town where things'll start a'poppin'.'

Getting the official permission he had hoped for, feeling safe because Pat Shephard would be between him and Roop Calmont when he arrived, Claude Sheen did a little half run down West Street. Not noticing his amused staff watching him from the hotel windows, he rushed to the schoolhouse to hammer on the door with the side of a clenched fist.

When Ellie Brookes opened the door to him her eyes were unusually sleepy, heavy-lidded. This gave her a sultriness that she hadn't previously possessed, but which Claude found added compellingly to her attractiveness. That wasn't the only noticeable difference in her. Ellie seemed poised, much more self-assured than ever before.

'Mr Sheen,' she greeted him.

She was always that formal, in spite of his insistent but futile campaign of courting. Claude was ever ready to devote his heart, his hotel, his life to her, but Ellie was as cool towards him now as she had been the the first time they'd met.

'Thank the Lord that you are safe, Miss Ellie,' he exclaimed.

'Whatever is the matter, Mr Sheen?' she gasped.

Claude Sheen hesitated to find words that would add urgency to his reply. He

61

glanced skywards. The sun was close to its zenith. Roop Calmont had been expected long before this, so he was sure to be along at any moment.

'Sheriff Decker's expecting an outlaw named Roop Calmont to ride into town looking for trouble, Miss Ellie,' he said, mystified by a puzzling but sweetly attractive little smile that played around her lips at the mention of Roop Calmont. 'I've got everything organized in town, and I'll take you along so that you can stay with Ida Cault in the store.'

Ellie, surprisingly unflustered when all the other women in town were unnerved by what was about to happen, had started to say something when there was a noisy disturbance just yards from them.

The branches of a giant cottonwood rattled and shook noisily. Then a man plummeted to the ground and lay flat on his back, puffing and groaning. The writhing, tubby body was that of Paul Landers, the recently arrived writer. Pat

Shephard, holding a rifle, and walking with the litheness of a wild animal, came over to look down at the fallen Landers.

'Is a rider coming?' the deputy sheriff asked tersely.

'Didn't see one,' Lander replied between what sounded like sobs of pain. Propping himself up in the dust on one elbow, massaging his back with the other hand, he went on, 'I got pins and needles in my leg, and when I shifted to get comfortable I fell out of the tree.'

Shephard called Lander a foul name that Claude Sheen fervently wished Miss Ellie Brookes had not been unfortunate enough to hear.

★   ★   ★

Having built a fire in the stove, Roop Calmont slid a skillet over the blaze, and sliced some bacon ready for frying. The aroma of cooking food stirred savagely at him to produce a hunger he

63

hadn't known about. Grasping a coffee pot, he walked over to the table. Nancy looked up at him dumbly.

When he had brought her round she had shrieked and shrunk back from him. Over and over again he had patiently repeated his name and that he was Clayton's brother. Eventually he got through to her, but his nearness had made her uneasy as he'd tenderly bathed the blood from her face, and slight tremors were still running through her now as he filled two mugs with coffee.

Though it was obvious what had happened to her, Roop hadn't asked any questions and neither had she volunteered any statement. Knowing that he would eventually have to learn the details, guilt caused him to delay as long as possible. If he hadn't succumbed to the lure of Ellie Brookes, then it was likely he'd have been here at the Double J and Nancy wouldn't have suffered her ordeal.

She spoke for the first time as he

placed a fried breakfast in front of her and sat opposite with his own plate on the table. Her voice was croaky from lack of use, and the bruising and swelling caused her to mumble until exercise freed out her facial muscles.

'What brought you here?'

'I heard of the trouble Clay was in, and came to help out.'

'How were you thinking of helping him?'

As she looked at him Roop saw the slight turn in her eye. He wondered if she'd had it before or if it was a result of the attack on her. Imagining her without the bruises and scratches on her face, and with the now tangled red hair brushed and tidy, he mentally complimented his brother on picking a real beauty.

'I'll tell you about it after we've eaten,' he assured her.

'I'd like to talk now,' she said, chewing the hot food cautiously because her swollen lips were sore. 'Clayton mentioned that he had a brother, but never told me anything about you. I'm sorry, you told me your name but it's gone clean out of my head.'

'That's understandable,' he said. 'I think you're very brave. My name's Roop.'

'I don't feel brave.' She glanced at the belt with its holstered .45 draped over the back of his chair, enquiring, 'Are you a gunman?'

'Something like that,' he confessed obliquely.

Reaching for the coffee pot, she started to say something but stopped when he got to the pot first and refilled both their mugs. Roop smiled at her, pleased that reaction from the attack was ebbing away. Nancy was tough as well as pretty, and was recovering real good. She was relaxing as she came to trust him.

'If you were about to ask me if I'm wanted by the law, the answer is no,' he said.

'I wouldn't have asked.' Nancy

pushed her wildly brushed hair back from her face, commenting to herself, 'I must tidy myself up.' Then she continued speaking to him. 'That's your business. But I would like to know how you intend to help Clayton.'

Pushing his empty plate from him, Roop took out the makings and asked her permission tacitly by raising his eyebrows. When Nancy nodded her consent he rolled a cigarette, remaining silent until it was alight and he had dragged in smoke.

'What I had in mind,' he then told her, 'was to break Clay out of jail late today. I told the sheriff, who's just a bit of a kid, that I'd be coming into town first light this morning: planning to go in later when he'd relaxed his vigilance,'

'What then?'

'I guess me and Clay would then have ridden off to find this Bailey *hombre*. We get him and Clay's in the clear. But now things have changed.'

Plainly having approved of his plan, Nancy frowningly asked, 'In what way have things changed?'

'What has happened to you changes things, Nancy. I don't intend to leave you here on your own. Can you talk about it? Was it one man?'

'Three,' she said in a whisper, lowering her head.

'Three men together are easier to find than a lone rider,' Roop said with a little nod of satisfaction. 'Did you hear any names mentioned, Nancy?'

'I'll never forget them or their names,' she said miserably. 'One called himself John G. Wheeler, the other was Mark Butterfield, and they called the third man, who was a Mexican, Snake.'

'I won't forget those names either,' Roop promised his sister-in-law.

'I'll be fine here, Roop,' she said, having enough confidence in him now to use his name. 'I want you and Clayton to go find Mitch Bailey.'

'We will,' he promised. 'I'll get Clay out of jail tonight. Then we'll come back here to fetch you, make the house secure, and you can ride out with us.'

Pleased at seeing relief flood through her, Roop stood, picking up the coffee pot. 'I'll make us some more coffee.'

'I don't want Clayton to see me like this.' An unhappy Nancy waved a hand to indicate her swollen face.

'I'll explain what happened. Break it to him real easy,' Roop told her.

'Thank you,' she said, grateful for his reassurance. 'Where do you think Bailey is?'

'Clay reckons he could be hiding out up in the San Jacinto hills, so we'll start looking there.'

'Do you think it will take long to find him, Roop?' she asked, obviously eager to get things moving.

'I'll let you know after I've caught up with John G. Wheeler, Mark Butterfield, and a greaser called Snake,' he replied flatly.

★ ★ ★

'Who is it?'

A whisper didn't come naturally to

69

old Matt Brown, and his query voiced through the locked door of the sheriff's office sounded like a shout in the night to Roop Calmont, who was pressed up against the door outside in the dark street.

'It's me, Decker,' Roop muttered. 'Open up.'

'What in tarnation you doing here this time of night, Sheriff?' the old man protested. 'By the horn spoons! Don't you think I'm capable of guarding a gosh-darned prisoner?'

'Just open up,' Roop ordered hoarsely. 'Roop Calmont's been seen in town.'

'Land sakes! Why the blazes didn't you say so in the first place?'

There was the rasping sound of bolts being drawn and, as a giving of the door signalled that the last one was being pulled, Roop hit the door with the full weight of his body. It crashed inwards, sending old Matt flying across the room to land sitting on the floor in a corner. The flame of an oil lamp on the desk danced crazily before sending up a protest in smoke and settling down. Closing and bolting the door fast, Roop turned to the old jailer.

'Just stay quiet and do as I say, old-timer.'

Putting a hand inside his jacket, Matt Brown warned, 'I've got a Bowie knife.'

'Careful you don't cut yourself,' Roop advised. 'Now, on your feet and fetch the key to the cage you've got my brother in.'

Clambering stiffly up off the floor, the old fellow issued another warning. 'I ought to tell you I was at the Battle of Gettysburg.'

'That's funny, I didn't see you there,' Roop told him laconically. 'Now stop with the mouth and start with the hands, old-timer. The key.'

'You wouldn't have spoken to me like that twenty years ago,' Matt grumbled, as he went over to open a drawer in a desk and pull out a bunch of keys.

Roop followed the old man out of the office and down the passageway that had iron bars on each side. Clayton was the only prisoner, and he stood in his cell, holding the bars of the door as Brown and Roop approached.

'Open up,' Roop ordered, and old Matt turned the big key in the lock and swung the door open outwards.

'We've got quite a walk to where I've left the horses,' Roop told Clayton quietly when they were out in the office.

'What about old Matt?' Clayton questioned. 'I don't want him hurt, Roop.'

Roop grabbed the old man by the arm. 'Listen to me, old-timer, and listen real good. You're going to let us out of that door, and close it behind us. Then I want to hear every bolt pushed home, and I'll be waiting out there, ready to blast your head off if you try to open the door. I'll be there long enough for my brother to get away. Remember, you've been warned.'

'I'll remember,' the old man nodded. 'I ain't fixing to get shot,'

'Ready,' Roop said tersely, and Matt Brown opened the door. 'That's wide enough. You first, Clay.'

Turning sideways to pass through the narrow gap, Clayton Calmont went out onto the street. His brother was close behind, turning to order Matt Brown in a harsh whisper, 'Close the door.'

But the old man had other plans. With a speed surprising in someone old and arthritic, he snatched the oil lamp from the desk and threw it hard out into the night. As the elderly jailer dived for safety in the dense new darkness, the lamp hit the road to spill flaming oil across the street. Like a brightly-lit fuse, a string of flame reached out to connect with the dry boarding of the sidewalk outside a haberdashery shop. The flames caught quickly and devoured the planking before eating their way up the walls of the shop.

The Calmont brothers were running, but the town was awakening as the fire spread, flames roaring so that the whole shop front was engulfed. Doors and windows were being opened.

A shout went up. 'Martha Gibbon's place is ablaze!'

Keeping to the shadows on the opposite side of the street to the fire, avoiding the people who had started to dash around at speed but aimlessly, Roop said to Clayton, 'The old fella did us a favour. I've got the horses hitched at the edge of town behind the schoolhouse. This fire is a useful diversion.'

But he soon found that he was mistaken. Things were more organized now. A chain of buckets had been set up, and water was being thrown over the burning shop when Matt Brown came on the scene, running down the street, firing a rifle into the air and shouting. 'Roop Calmont's broke his brother out of the calaboose. They're heading for the bottom of town on foot!'

The two brothers started to run. Behind them they heard Pat Shephard's voice shout a question. 'Which way, Matt?'

'Down West Street, Pat, down West Street.'

A slug from the deputy sheriff's rifle smacked into the corner of a building, just above Clayton's head. They kept running, but there were more shots, the bullets whining too close for them to stay exposed on the street. Pulling his brother by the arm, Roop turned into a gap between buildings. They sped through the darkness, coming out into a waste area behind the buildings.

'That way.' A pleased Roop Clayton swung his hand to indicate the dark bulk of the schoolhouse.

'Where are the horses?' Clayton asked, breathing heavily.

'Between two cottonwoods behind the scho — ' Roop was answering when a bullet tore away the collar of his jacket. He wasn't hurt, but the force had spun him round and he had to get his bearings again.

That shot was close, and it had come

from behind. But Roop was still hopeful of making it. As they moved on, Clayton dropped to one knee but quickly came up again.

'You hurt, Clay?' an anxious Roop asked.

'Hit in the foot,' an annoyed Clayton replied. 'Nothing serious. Let's get to them horses.'

By now the blaze was lighting up the town, and it produced two silhouettes, both holding rifles, up ahead by the schoolhouse.

It was hopeless. They were trapped between Shephard coming up behind them, and whoever it was, probably Decker and somebody else, coming towards them. Stopping, Roop pulled his brother into an alcove beside him.

'Sorry, Clay, but it didn't work.' Taking a spare gun from the waistband of his trousers and passing it to Clayton, he drew his own. 45. 'We'll take as many of them with us as we can.'

Not accepting the six-shooter,

Clayton said, 'I don't want no killing on my behalf. You make a run for it, Roop, and I'll give myself up.'

'I'm not about to run, and you're not giving yourself up,' Roop said grimly, his .45 held at the ready. 'That little woman of yours is expecting us back.'

That sounded good, but there was no hope of escape. The two brothers couldn't see those hunting them now, but small sounds in the darkness warned that they were out there, and closing in.

'Are you out there, Roop?' a woman's voice called softly.

Startled, Roop looked around quickly to see Ellie Brookes had opened a side door in the schoolhouse. She stood waiting, shielding the sparse light from the lantern she was holding.

With a hand on his brother's arm to guide him, Roop ran for the door, Clayton limping at his side. They went into the schoolhouse fast, and Ellie swiftly closed and bolted the door.

She put a finger to her lips, before

whispering, 'We must be quiet. You can stay in here until they've gone.'

Reaching out a hand to give Ellie's shoulder a squeeze to express his thanks, Roop had a sudden thought and had to abort the oath he was about to give voice to. 'The horses. They'll find them.'

'No,' Ellie whispered. 'I found them out there and put them in the woodshed. It's empty this time of year.'

'You're sure a good girl, Ellie,' Roop breathed gratefully.

'You of all people know I'm not good, Roop Calmont,' she said, and he was sure she'd be blushing in the dark.

Then they all tensed as someone rapped on the main door of the schoolhouse. 'Are you in there, Miss Ellie?'

'It's Claude Sheen.' She leaned close enough to Roop for him to breathe in her perfume as she reached out to stay his gunhand as it went to his holster. 'He's no danger. I'll get rid of him.'

Holding her lantern high, Ellie went

to the door but didn't open it. Sheen called again, 'Are you in there, Miss Ellie?'

'Yes.'

'Are you all right? There's been a break-out up at the jail, and the Calmont brothers headed this way.'

'I haven't seen anything of them,' Ellie said. 'Sparks from that fire were blowing this way, and I'm checking to see that the schoolhouse is safe.'

'Do you want me to help, Miss Ellie?'

'No, thank you. Everything is fine.'

'Good,' Claude Sheen called, 'Then I'll get away to join the others. Decker's switched the search for the Calmonts over to North Street.'

'That's good news for you two,' Ellie smiled as she came back to them, shock on her face as she held the lantern to get a better look at Clayton's foot, which was leaking blood. 'You're hurt. Take your boot off and I'll fetch some bandages.'

'No.' Roop stopped her from leaving. 'If Clay takes his boot off he won't be able to get it back on. We've got to go while the going's good.'

They went out in the night, leading their horses out of the woodshed while Ellie held the door open. She helped the injured Clayton to mount, and, ready to ride away, Roop leaned down from the saddle to extend a hand to her.

Taking the hand in both of hers, Ellie said forlornly, 'Don't you go forgetting me, Roop Calmont.'

4

Most folk have a preconceived idea of judges. Those prepared to sit in judgment on their fellow men were thought to over-indulge in food and liquor. Folk saw them as big, bulging men with most of their excess weight carried round their waists. That general view was really appreciated by Judge Jason Landseer, who was as lean and mean as a starving coyote caught up in a drought. Landseer always delighted in the shock his appearance gave people who were expecting someone more distinguished-looking. Alighting from the stagecoach in Pine Notch had been no exception. The inhabitants, dismissing him as some gun salesman or whiskey drummer, looked past Landseer in anticipation of seeing the judge they were expecting still sitting in the coach. It was the same old pattern but with one difference: Judge Landseer was just as lean as he ever was, but he was a whole lot meaner because of the bungling law officers in the town. Having travelled a great distance to preside over the trial of a cattle rustler, he had arrived to learn that the accused had flown the coop, as it were. None of this surprised Landseer, who had naught but contempt for a town that had appointed an obviously decadent boy as sheriff.

Out of duty, the judge had invited that inept sheriff to his room in the town's Peak View Hotel. A long-haired deputy US marshal who looked to Landseer to be more menacing than most of the killers who had stood trial in front of him, had arrived in town round about the same time as the judge. The deputy marshal had come along with the sheriff.

Decker immediately defended himself. 'There weren't nothing could be done that night, Judge Landseer, not with Roop Calmont taking a hand in things.'

'I'm used to hearing excuses from the accused in court, not officers of the law, Sheriff Decker,' Landseer said bitingly. 'But, having said that, I am not unacquainted with the reputation of Rupert Calmont, However, I confess that this Clayton Calmont is unknown to me. You were the arresting officer, Marshal Falk?'

'Yes, Judge,' Falk replied. 'Clayton is Roop Calmont's brother, but is unlike him in every way. Clayton is a married man, a law-abiding rancher.'

'Law abiding!' Landseer half-shouted in his indignation. 'Correct me if I am wrong, but you arrested that man on a charge of rustling. Was it your intention to waste the time of the judiciary?'

'No. There is evidence against him, but I don't believe it would have stood up in court.'

'Then why arrest him?'

'I did my job, Judge, then left it to you to do yours.'

This taciturn fellow was being insolent, Landseer was certain of that but couldn't do anything about it right then. It would be a different matter in the near future. He sternly addressed the two lawmen.

'Clayton Calmont has a charge of escaping from custody to answer as well as cattle-theft. Roop Calmont, a highly dangerous man in my estimation, was both the instigator and principal force behind Clayton Calmont's escape, an escape in which property in this town was fired, endangering the lives of the citizens. I know Roop Calmont of old, and there's no place in this territory for him or his kind.'

Judge Landseer glared at Decker and Falk in turn before going on. 'Sheriff Decker, Marshal Falk, I give you both fair warning that I shall return to this town in three months' time, when I shall expect Clayton Calmont to be in custody awaiting trial. It would seem to me that the terms of capture dead or alive applies to Roop Calmont, so either he will be standing in court beside his brother, or I will be presented with proof of his death. Is that clearly understood?'

'Yes, sir,' Sheriff Decker said respectfully.

'I'm leaving town tonight to go after them, Judge,' Falk announced.

'Roop Calmont, dead or alive,' Landseer issued a reminder.

'I'll do whatever has to be done,' Falk said, before walking out of the room without another word.

* * *

The ageing doctor's wrinkled-skinned hands shook as they gently explored Clayton Calmont's ankle. Instead of the wound improving over several weeks, the joint had swollen to more than twice its size, and was badly discoloured. With his wife and brother standing looking on, Clayton lay on a bed in the St James Hotel, which stood on the main street of Las Animas. They had come a long way, with Clayton suffering all the time he had been in the saddle. The diligently searching Roop had called at every saloon they passed to ask questions about Mitch Bailey. Nancy felt sure that Roop had also been enquiring about the men who had attacked her. Clayton had taken it badly. Though not a man given to anger, she knew that her husband was fretting because his injured ankle prevented him from avenging her. Her hope was that by the time his injury had healed, Clayton's thirst for revenge would have abated. He wasn't a fighting man, and she'd rather those who'd abused her got away with it than she lose her husband.

'The bone has been chipped,' the doctor reported as he stood back from the bed. 'Something has to be done about that swelling. I'll call round in the morning to bleed the ankle.'

'I'll be able to use it then, Doc?' Clayton asked hopefully.

'You'll be able to limp, but best keep

your weight off it for a couple of weeks, then you'll be able to get around. But it will be months before that leg will work properly for you.'

Her husband's frustration at hearing this was obvious to Nancy. Roop paid the old doctor and she showed him to the door, where he reversed the usual social procedure by introducing himself as he left instead of on arrival.

'Dr Levins, at your service, ma'am. I specialize in gunshot wounds.' Levins took a meaningful look at the hard-faced Roop, who leaned with a shoulder against the wall, his thumbs hooked in his gunbelt. 'I think perhaps you may have further need of my professional assistance before you ride out of Las Animas.'

Closing the door behind Dr Levins, Nancy hurried back to the bed. Clayton's usually darktanned face was white. She knew that not only had the long ride they'd made been agony for him, but he was also suffering from not being able to play an active part in the search for Bailey. Though she doubted that Clayton resented playing second fiddle to his brother, the fact that he had to made him feel inferior.

'Let's get you on your feet and we'll go down and get ourselves some chow,' Roop said, putting out an arm with the intention of helping his brother up off the bed.

'No,' Clayton said. 'You take Nancy down to the dining-room, Roop. I don't feel much like eating, but you could bring me something back up if it isn't any trouble.'

Hearing this made Nancy hate herself for the flash of disloyalty she experienced. A surge of joy at the thought of being alone with Roop had been both momentary and involuntary, but it also distressed her. It was understandable in that the two Calmont brothers were very much alike in many ways, but Nancy was honest with herself and accepted that there was more to it than that. The loving, kind, caring and considerate

Clayton was an ideal husband. While aware that the harsher life led by his brother meant that Roop would lack Clayton's finer feelings, being in Roop's company gave her a sense of security such as she had never known with her husband. Contrarily, there was an element of danger in Roop. Even though Nancy knew that he was no threat to her, she was disturbed nevertheless.

Realizing all this put Nancy on her guard, and she purposefully developed and maintained an air of detachment from Roop as they sat at a table together in the hotel's dining-room downstairs. The place was crowded, which allowed her to keep the conversation light.

Aware, not for the first time, of Roop's constant vigilance, she knew that he had seen the tall man wearing a star pinned to his breast before she did. The lawman entered the dining-room with a contrived casualness, eyes scanning the occupants. When his gaze came to their table he took off his hat and headed in their direction.

'There's a sheriff coming towards us,' she told Roop, knowing that he already knew this, but, prompted by nervousness, or it could have been fear, it brought her relief to speak.

'A town marshal,' he corrected her.

Then the lawman was beside them, a lanky figure wearing two gunbelts and with a holstered gun at each hip. He addressed them in an unmistakable Texas accent. 'Evening, folks. Forgive me if I'm interrupting your dinner. I'm Tex Singer, town marshal here in Las Animas.'

'We're just about through,' Nancy said.

'What can we do for you, Marshal?' Roop asked civilly.

'Could be that I can do something for you,' Singer replied. 'You look to me like the fella people in town say has been asking questions.'

'That's me, I'm Roop Calmont, What can you tell me about Mitch Bailey?'

Roop enquired as he pushed a spare chair out from the table with his foot. 'Take a chair, Marshal.'

Pushing the chair round with his own foot, the marshal sat on it reverse-fashion, folded arms resting on the chairback as he said, 'I can't tell you nothing about Bailey, except that he's holed up somewhere in the San Jacinto hills with a gang of outlaws. Bailey was here in Las Animas for a spell. He didn't give me any trouble, but he's bad news. Last I heard he was seen riding with a real wild bunch, so my advice is to keep away from him, Calmont.'

'If it's all the same to you, Marshal Singer,' Roop drawled, 'I'm not looking for advice, but information.'

Shrugging, Singer said, 'The advice is there, take it or leave it. But it'll interest you that there's a guy in town in the company of another white man and a Mex. The guy calls himself John G. Wheeler.'

Nancy looked sharply at Roop. She'd guessed right. He had been seeking the men who had attacked her as well as Bailey. She could sense he was a little troubled by her scrutiny. But he looked eagerly at the town marshal.

'Where can I find this man, Marshal?'

'Wheeler has a card game going every night in Mendoza's in the Mexican quarter.'

'Thanks, Marshal,' Roop said gratefully. 'I'll call on him.'

'There's just one more thing before I leave you and your lady, Calmont,' Singer said. 'I run a tight town. It ain't easy because we've got troublemakers here and all sorts passing through all the time.'

'Are you warning me off, Marshal?' Roop asked, a touch of menace creeping into his voice.

'No, I never come between a man and his business, but I don't want you interfering with mine either,' the marshal answered. 'It's like this, Calmont: when I make my rounds of a night I never get to Mendoza's place until after ten o'clock. Whatever business you got with this John G. Wheeler, get it over with before ten so's it don't make extra work for me.'

'You've got it, Marshal,' Roop agreed with a pleased smile.

'And whatever that business is of yours, get out of town soon as you've settled it,' the marshal said as he stood, made a respectful half salute at Nancy, then turned and walked away.

'Now there's a man who understands how to administer the law,' Roop told Nancy with a smile when Singer was out of earshot. 'I'll have the cook rustle up some grub to take up to Clay, then we'll go call on John G. Wheeler.'

'But we are after Mitch Bailey,' Nancy protested.

Roop looked deeply into her eyes, and a thrill shuddered through her for a moment as it seemed he was about to take her hand. He spoke very softly. 'We'll get to Bailey, but the men who hurt you are here in this town, Nancy, and I can't leave without paying them for what they did to you.'

'But . . . ' Nancy started to object but her mind was too busy contemplating Roop's obvious feelings for her to supply her with words. Clearing her head by thinking of Clayton, she managed to say, 'I'd rather we went back to Clayton now, and the three of us left Las Animas in the morning.'

'We'll leave in the morning,' Roop assured her, 'but I want you to come with me to Mendoza's tonight.'

The thought of seeing Wheeler again appalled and terrified Nancy. 'Why do you want me with you, Roop?'

'I have never killed a man without telling him why, Nancy,' Roop replied. 'I want Wheeler and the others to see you, then they'll know why they are about to die.'

What was a warm evening suddenly turned cold for Nancy. Roop Calmont spoke of killing as unemotionally as his brother talked about getting feed in for the winter. The powerful magnetism Roop had held for her such a short time ago, began to wane fast. Nancy wished it would disappear completely, but it refused to do so.

'Let's make a move,' Roop said.

⋆　⋆　⋆

'It certainly is a splendid night, Miss Ellie,' Claude Sheen commented, pausing to offer the schoolteacher his arm as they came out of the New Theatre into warm but pleasantly refreshing night air.

Ellie demurely agreed, laying a small white hand lightly, very lightly, on her escort's proffered arm. It had been a most enjoyable evening. *The Banker's Daughter* was a play she had long wanted to see, and the Nellie Boyd Dramatic Company of New York had performed it excellently. In the theatre it had felt right to be at Claude Sheen's side. He was kindness itself, the complete gentleman, the ideal companion for an evening of culture. At first unsure whether to accept his invitation, fearing Claude would regard her acceptance as the start of a relationship, Ellie was now glad that she had. In fact, caught up in a romantic atmosphere generated by the players on stage, she had welcomed Claude Sheen's veiled suggestions that there would be other occasions on which they would be together. Though here in the present, he was a reminder of her past; Claude Sheen was representative of the stable, polite and intellectual society in which she had been raised.

Yet all that was changing fast out here in the stillness of a New Mexico night. The sun was down, the last weak streaks of red from it flecking the western sky. With the moon not yet up, a myriad of stars had claimed their sparkling place in the heavens. For all its tranquillity there was a wildness, a savagery lying dormant in the night. Ellie could sense it, feel it to the extent that she was stirred. To know that Roop was sharing this same sky brought him close to her.

'I do hope that Nancy and Mr Calmont are safe somewhere,' she said as Claude Sheen walked her slowly towards the schoolhouse. hoping to lure him into mentioning Roop. Her ploy was successful.

'I am sure that they are,' Sheen assured her. 'Clayton is a stalwart fellow who will ensure no harm befalls his wife. I pray that brother of his won't spoil any chance that they have of returning here to Pine Notch and settling that ridiculous accusation of rustling.'

'Do you think that Mr Clayton's brother . . . oh dear, what is his name . . . ?'

'Roop,' Claude Sheen, a bachelor ignorant of the wiles of women in love, readily replied.

'Roop, yes, that's it, Roop,' Ellie repeated the name, savouring it each time she said it, finding it more thrilling verbalized than when she ran it silently and constantly through her mind. 'In what way do you feel this Roop might spoil it for them, Mr Sheen?'

'To be frank, Miss Ellie, I don't think that he will have the chance to do so,' Claude said confidently. 'While accepting that Roop Calmont has quite a formidable reputation, I hardly see him as a match for the man who has gone off after him, Orland Falk.'

'The deputy US marshal who arrested Mr Calmont?'

'That's right Miss Ellie. If I had to have one of them tracking me down, heaven forbid, I would choose it to be Orland Falk.'

Ellie's heart felt as cold as ice in her breast. Roop Calmont had seemed invincible to her, but now she was terribly worried that Claude Sheen could be right. What if that quiet and mysterious lawman should gun down Roop?

They were at the schoolhouse now, and Claude Sheen laid a soft hand on top of the one she had on his arm.

'This has been a wonderful night for me, Miss Ellie.'

'I've had a delightful time, Mr Sheen.'

'It both pleases me to hear you say that, and gives me the courage to say that there are matters I wish to discuss, things that I want to say to you, Miss Ellie.'

In the theatre she would probably have accommodated him, but that was a thousand years ago before the night sent the thought of Roop Calmont pulsing through her body.

'You are a charming man, Mr Sheen, and I don't wish to appear rude,' she said, 'but I am so tired, and I fear that the tobacco smoke in the theatre may be bringing on one of my headaches.'

'Forgive me for being so inconsiderate, Miss Ellie,' he said contritely, adding hesitantly, 'In bidding you a very goodnight, might I be so bold as to enquire if you are opposed to at some time hearing what I have to say?'

'Indeed I am not, sir,' she said with a coquettish smile.

* * *

'May I suggest a game of chance, gentlemen? Permit me to introduce myself as former Sergeant John G. Wheeler of Company C, 14th Pennsylvania Cavalry. I was honoured at Stone River, Tennessee, when I received a medal for Gallantry in Action, and I would be highly honoured right now if some of you gentlemen will join me in breaking open a brand new pack of cards and starting a game.'

Nancy heard every word spoken by Wheeler. She stood on the sidewalk with Roop, close to the doors of Mendoza's saloon. Clayton didn't know anything about her attackers being in town. Roop had convinced him that he was taking her to buy spare horses for the ride into the San Jacinto hills.

Wheeler was standing inside with his back to the bar, Seeing him brought back terrible memories, but Nancy didn't realize how tense she was until she gave a little jump when Roop spoke.

'Which one is Butterfield?'

Nancy scanned the bar, screwing her eyes up so as to see better through the haze of tobacco smoke. This was the Mexican quarter of town, but most of the men in the saloon were white. She spotted the dirty, unshaven Butterfield standing just a few feet away from Wheeler.

'The man wearing the battered bowler hat,' she said, surprised at the steadiness of her voice.

'And Snake?'

'That's him, with his arm round that Mexican woman.'

Studying the scene inside for a moment, Roop then instructed, 'Go on in, Nancy. Walk over to Wheeler, but don't get too close. Stop as soon as he recognizes you. Don't worry, I won't be

101

far away from you.'

Pushing the door inwards, Nancy, feeling terribly afraid, entered the saloon. All eyes turned her way, interest having the men straighten up at the astonishing sight of an attractive red-head in such a low place. The saloon women, the majority of them dark-skinned, glared at her jealously. She was aware of Roop following her in, but he had gone off at an angle to walk parallel to her as she went along close to the bar.

Realizing that something unusual was going on, Wheeler turned his head in her direction. His eyes widened and bulged in shock when he recognized her. Then he recovered to return to being his bombastic self, a grin spreading over his face. Wheeler seemed to be under the illusion that she had sought him out for a reason far from that of revenge.

'Wheeler!'

As Roop spoke the name, Nancy looked to where he stood, facing

102

Wheeler, his arms at his sides, seemingly relaxed.

'And who might you be, sir?' Wheeler affably enquired. 'Perchance an old comrade from Company C? If that is the case, then do please forgive me not remembering your na — '

'Do you remember this woman, Wheeler?' Roop interrupted.

Nancy noticed that Butterfield was apparently unarmed. But Snake, his arm still round the waist of the Mexican woman, was moving her and himself sideways, closer to Roop.

'I can't say that I know her, sir,' Wheeler replied conversationally. 'But she is a remarkable-looking woman, sir. It is a matter for regret that I can't recall having met her, sir.'

'That's so,' Roop said flatly, 'because she's the reason you are about to die.'

Nancy wanted to shout a warning as the Mexican woman — she and Snake now close to Roop — picked up a glass half full of red-eye from a table. It was plain that she was going to throw the

103

alcohol into Roop's eyes, but Nancy froze and her vocal chords wouldn't work.

Horrified, she watched the woman pull her arm back ready to toss the contents of the glass at Roop, as the man called Snake sneakily placed his right hand on the butt of his holstered gun. The whole place was held in a taut silence. Nancy was close to collapse because Roop seemed oblivious to what Snake and the woman were preparing to do.

Then Nancy had difficulty in keeping track of what happened because it occurred so fast. The Mexican woman's arm jerked forwards, the whiskey sloshing up close to the rim of the glass. But Roop had drawn his .45. Lashing out with it sideways he caught the woman across the forehead with the barrel. There was a sickening, cracking sound as her skull was split open and she dropped lifelessly to the floor. Snake had drawn his gun, but he hadn't levelled it when Roop fired. The bullet caught the Mexican just above the bridge of the nose and his face imploded.

Turning, bringing his Colt to bear on Wheeler, who had made no attempt to go for his gun, but stood immobile and ashen-faced, Roop let his own .45 slide back into its holster with the intention of provoking Wheeler to draw on him.

But Wheeler pre-empted the move. Nancy heard her own hoarse cry of alarm as Wheeler drew while Roop's .45 was dropping into the holster. A concerted gasp of astonishment ran through the saloon as Roop swiftly drew once again and fired. Wheeler released a shot that harmlessly sprayed up sawdust as he sank to the floor, where he lay writhing and groaning.

An elderly rancher looked sadly down at Wheeler and remarked, 'A belly-shot. There ain't nothing so painful, and there ain't no getting over them.'

That was what Roop had planned, Nancy realized. He wanted Wheeler to die in agony for what he had done to her. Neither was he finished yet. Roop was facing Butterfield, who stood with his open hands spread wide, shaking with fright as he pleaded, 'You can see I ain't armed, mister.'

Looking swiftly down at Wheeler, whose fingers still held his gun tightly as he convulsed, Roop callously stamped on the dying man's wrist. The fingers flew open, releasing the gun, which Roop scooped up and tossed to Butterfield. A surprised Butterfield, not really aware of what was happening, instinctively caught the gun. As he fumbled awkwardly with it, Roop fired. The shot came from so close that it blasted the right side of Butterfield's face away.

Feeling sick, Nancy was gagging as she felt Roop's arm go round her supportingly. It helped a little, but the acrid smell of cordite bit deep inside of her nostrils, and the violent deaths all around had been too much for her.

Tex Singer came in then. Striding up

he looked at the three dead men. He frowned as he saw the broken-headed corpse of the Mexican woman. He swung his head to Roop. 'You said you had a score to settle, Calmont. I wasn't expecting a goddamned massacre.'

'Neither was I, Marshal.'

Hefting the rifle he held in a half-threatening movement to support his words, Singer said, 'Get yourself and your woman out of town.'

'We'll be gone at first light,' Roop promised.

'No you won't, you'll leave right now, Calmont,' the town marshal said.

5

High on a hill outside of Las Animas, Deputy US Marshal Orland Falk pulled his horse in as a creaking wagon laden with four coffins made of rough-hewn wood passed by. Sitting in the saddle, he watched a desolate scene unfold as the lone wagon entered a hilltop cemetery. There were no accompanying mourners, just the driver of the wagon and four gloomy-faced men who were obviously there simply to bury the deceased. The watching Falk wondered. Death, or rather the way death affects the living, always fascinated him. So many times he had seen raised passions lead to an explosion of gunfire that was followed by an unearthly silence, and often the profound regret of those who had pulled the triggers.

With the ringing of shovels against

hard ground in his ears, he rode on into a town that seemed to be still firmly held in the grip of whatever had brought about the four deaths. People were moving about, but in a subdued manner, and an eerie quiet that hugged the warm air. In the blinding white sunshine of midday, Las Animas was squalid, unlovely, unwelcoming.

Pacing his horse slowly among the main street, Falk studied the buildings on each side. Seeing the town marshal's office to his right, he rode over to it. He had one foot out of the stirrup when the door opened and a man wearing a silver star on his chest and two six-guns on his hips stepped out.

'This ain't a good day for visiting, stranger,' the man with the star said belligerently. 'In fact, it's too bad a day for you to even think about getting down from that brone.'

'Seems you're telling me to ride back out of town,' Falk said easily.

'I reckon I am telling you to pull foot, stranger.'

'Who's telling me?' Falk mildly enquired.

'What difference does that make? You're going anyway.'

'I'd still like to know who's telling me.'

'There's always one ornery cuss.' The man with the star released an exasperated sigh. 'I'm the town marshal, Tex Singer.'

'Then I guess we're in the same business, Singer. I'm Deputy US Marshal Orland Falk.'

Giving the sidewalk a kick with the heel of his boot, an embarrassed Singer said, 'Well, don't that beat all! Light down, Marshal. I'm sure sorry about the way I met you.'

'It fitted in with the town,' Falk said, pulling a face as he took a look around, swinging down out of the saddle.

'Don't be too hasty judging the place,' Singer advised. 'Around about twilight Las Animas loses just about all of its ugliness.'

'I won't wait to find out, if you won't

be offended, Singer.'

Singer laughed. 'Can't say I blame you. You've come at a bad time, Falk. We've just had four killings in town.'

'I saw the burying as I rode in,' Falk said as he tied the reins of his horse to the rail. 'I'm looking for a man by the name of Clayton Calmont, Singer.'

'Well, if that don't beat all!' An incredulous town marshal repeated his earlier exclamation as he gaped at Falk, wide-eyed. 'It was a Calmont that did the killing here. But he wasn't Clayton, he was Roop. A tough-looking cuss with fair hair, worn kinda long, something like your own.'

'That's Clayton's brother,' a puzzled Falk frowned. 'Was he alone?'

'No. Had his woman with him, a redhead, a real grand-looking calico.'

'That's Clayton's wife.'

'Looks like there were some shecoonery going on,' Singer commented. 'I only saw one Calmont, and that was Roop.'

'Is he still in town, Singer?'

'No, he lit out for the San Jacinto hills,' the town marshal answered. 'Reckons as how he was looking for some man named Bailey.'

'Mitch Bailey?'

'That's the *hombre*. You after Bailey, too?'

'No,' Falk replied, 'just Clayton Calmont. Had him in jail, but a fool kid of a sheriff lost him. I guess he's with brother Roop, even though you didn't see him.'

'Could be. I can find out up at the hotel,' the town marshal said. 'Listen, Falk, I was just about to go across the street to get some chow. I'll stand you a meal, pardner, and I'll tell you all I know about this Roop Calmont. He sure caused me some problems. Land sakes! One of them he killed here was a woman.'

'A woman?' a surprised Falk queried as he crossed the street with Singer.

'I'll tell you all about it inside,' the town marshal said as they reached a tall, many-windowed building.

112

Stopping before stepping on to the sidewalk to tilt his head back and look up at the house, Falk remarked. 'This doesn't look like an eating-place to me, Singer.'

'This is Nellie Swift's place,' the town marshal grinned. 'It's a whorehouse. You got any objection, Falk?'

'That depends on what's being offered.'

'Just the best food in town.'

'Then I have no objection,' Falk solemnly replied.

★　★　★

To describe the place as a settlement would be to exaggerate. Situated in a dip some twenty miles into the San Jacinto hills, it was a collection of low and misshapen sod buildings. Dogs ran crazily around them in fragmented patterns as they rode in, barking and yelping annoyingly. The air held a mixture of many smells that totalled to a putrid stench that made Nancy turn up the collar of her coat, bowing her head to use the material as a filter to breathe through. Clayton rode on her left, his ankle now just about healed. On her right, the ever-watchful Roop had his rifle lying propped on the saddlehorn in front of him. Smoke rose from some of the dingy buildings, twisting but going straight up through the windless air. There were signs of life, but no people. The sound of a trumpet played in the rising and falling Mexican style came through the doorless opening of the largest building. Roop used his horse to nudge their mounts in that direction.

Holding his rifle when they dismounted, he took it with him as they walked to the open doorway. Putting himself in a position to enter first, Roop told them in hushed tones, 'We don't know what to expect in here, so be ready for anything.'

Nancy gave a nod to say that she understood. Clayton moved protectively behind her, covering her back should danger come unexpectedly from behind. It was a move that, among many other things, Roop had taught him since the three of them had been riding together. She had learned to trust Roop, even though she hadn't fully got over the way he had exploded into action in Las Animas. She had no qualms over his killing of Wheeler and the other two men to avenge her, but the woman he'd had no option but to hit, worried Nancy. They hadn't spoken of the woman, both of them keen to avoid the subject, but Nancy felt sure that the blow to the head had killed her.

She stepped in through the doorway behind Roop. It was dark, smoky and smelly inside. A mangy cur brushed past their legs, circled the dirt floor once, then lay down to curl up and instantly go to sleep. The trumpet playing faltered and then stopped. The musician, a young Mexican, placed the instrument on the bench beside him. The whites of his large eyes seemed luminous in the half light as he looked suspiciously at them.

There was a rough counter to their right, and tables and chairs were spread haphazardly around. The only others present in addition to the trumpet player was a Mexican couple, both grossly overweight, sitting together at a far table. As Roop walked further into the building, the man got up and waddled over to go behind the counter. He had a heavy black moustache that made the slightly protruding teeth below it look brilliantly white.

'Tequila,' the Mexican said like it was a foregone conclusion, and he looked perplexed when Roop used a shake of his head to refuse.

Having never been so hungry in her life, and although put off by the dirty appearance of the place, Nancy was relieved to hear Roop ask for food.

'Si, señor.'

'What have you got?'

'Succotash, señor.'

'That'll do,' Roop nodded.

'Tequila?' The Mexican made it a

question this time.

'No, we'll have water; don't worry, I'm willing to pay for it,' Roop said, as the woman got up from her chair to go behind the counter and shift pots on to a stove. Roop added, 'I'm looking for a man.'

The Mexican's sudden, high-pitched laugh reminded Nancy of the man who had come to the Double J with Wheeler. She shivered.

'Every *Americano* who comes here asks me about this man or that man,' the Mexican stopped laughing to complain. '*Madre di Dios, amigo*, there are more than two thousand desperados roaming the San Jacinto hills. Which one would you like me to find for you, *muy amigo?*'

'Forget it,' Roop said, ushering Nancy and Clayton towards a table as the efforts of the Mexican woman produced an aroma of cooking food.

'What is succotash?' Nancy asked Roop when they were seated.

'It's an Indian dish, Nancy, a soup

made of corn, beans and salt pork.'

'Sounds good,' she said, with a smile at her husband.

Clayton didn't smile back. He had become more and more depressed as time passed. Nancy was aware that he was regretting having left the jail in Pine Notch. Clayton saw their search as a hopeless one, and was convinced that he would have been proved innocent had he stood trial. Neither Roop nor she shared that optimism, but they didn't tell Clayton that. It worried Nancy that, in what appeared to be a perfectly natural process, as her husband withdrew from her, so did she and his brother become closer.

With his big eyes cautiously watching the man and woman behind the counter, the trumpet player leaned a little closer to Roop to ask, 'What is the name of the *hombre* you seek, *muchacho*?'

'Bailey, Mitch Bailey. Do you know such a man, Pedro?'

118

'Sanchez,' the Mexican corrected him, still furtively watching the couple behind the counter. 'I might know him, but my head aches so that I cannot think.'

'Will that help you to think, Sanchez?' Roop asked, placing a half eagle on the table in the Mexican's reach.

Giving the five-dollar gold coin an indifferent look, Sanchez replied unhappily, 'My head hurts very much, *muchacho*.'

Using a forefinger to retrieve the half eagle, Roop replaced it with an eagle. Taking the ten-dollar coin, Sanchez permitted himself a smile. 'Now I remember. *Señor* Bailey, he ride with the great El Toro.'

'Who's that?' Clayton tersely asked his brother.

'El Toro, bandit leader, rustler, murderer and horse-thief; could be said to run these hills, Clay. El Toro is a powerful man.' Roop answered his brother before questioning

Sanchez. 'Where is El Toro now, Sanchez?'

'In Rosarita, *muchacho*.'

The Mexican woman carried plates of steaming food across to their table; at her approach Sanchez pulled away and fell silent. All three of them ate hungrily. When Nancy had eaten enough to take the sharp edge off her hunger, she asked Roop about Rosarita.

'It's El Toro's headquarters, Nancy,' he replied.

'How long will it take us to get there?'

'Two weeks at the most,' Roop said. 'We'll get moving once we've eaten. We find Bailey, Clay, and you'll be back on your ranch, in the clear.'

'Fine,' Clayton said unenthusiastically.

Sanchez leaned over to Roop with a cautionary word. 'There are many dangers between here and Rosarita, *muchacho*.'

It had been a long while since Pine Notch had seen a wedding, and its citizens made the most of Ellie Brookes' and Claude Sheen's big day. The pretty Ellie was a blushing bride, but not for the right reasons. She was pregnant, and it had begun to show. Having the good sense not to wear the traditional white, Ellie wore a brown dress. On her head was a crown of orange-blossom. They were married in the schoolroom by the minister who'd moved into town only three weeks previously. The Nightingale twins, two of Ellie's pupils, were bridesmaids, while Derek Decker and an acutely self-conscious Pat Shephard were groomsmen.

At the reception, held in Claude's hotel and attended by just about everyone in town, the calls of congratulations were vastly outnumbered by guarded whispers. The more malicious of the women had done some counting to pin-point the evening Claude had escorted Ellie to the theatre as the conception date. Yet even the gossiping hags of Pine Notch couldn't believe that Claude Sheen, an absolute gentleman, could have behaved so badly.

With Matt Brown, who had a hand in just about everything that happened in town, playing the fiddle, the youngsters had whirled around the floor to the tune of 'Jim Crack Corr'. Now the older folk, with the bride and groom taking the lead, were enjoying a waltz. On the floor, with music and movement precluding any chance of them being overheard, Ellie told Claude for the hundredth time that she would one day tell him the name of the man who was the true father of their child.

'I have no need to know,' Claude smiled, as for the hundredth time he repeated his answer. 'Having you as my wife is so wonderful that I cannot bother my mind with anything else.'

Ellie didn't experience happiness but felt secure in the arms of her new husband. She knew how lucky she was to have Claude Sheen. Not only had he rescued her from a plight that would have meant losing her job and leaving town, but he loved her so much that he was willing to tarnish his own reputation by letting the Pine Notch people assume the child she carried was his.

'You are a good man, Claude Sheen,' she told him.

'I'm a happy man,' he said, tightening the arms he had round her.

Finding that her tension was eased as she moved to the rhythm of the music, Ellie found herself thinking of Roop Calmont. This was something she had been doing constantly, but this time she was able to tell herself that the wild man didn't matter to her.

Minutes later, as the dance ended, she was starkly aware that she had lied to herself. She realized, and suffered a massive guilt towards Claude Sheen because of it, that when Roop Calmont came back for her, as he had promised, she would leave her husband and Pine

Notch without giving either a second thought.

★ ★ ★

Dusk was changing the greys and greens of the canyon into an undulating purple sea as they followed the trail into it. Five days and nights had passed by since they'd had a meal in the lowly *cantina*. Since then they had eaten only cold meat from the deer that Roop had killed and cooked four days ago. They had the makings for coffee, but Roop had declared it would be dangerous to light a fire. Clayton was taking more of a part in things now, adding to Nancy's guilt at having occasionally pondered on whether her husband's non-violent attitude to life had really been disguised cowardice. Far from welcoming these thoughts, Nancy could tell that Clayton's childlike reliance on his brother helped promote them.

That morning a rider had topped a rise behind them. The mounted man

124

was distant, but both Nancy and Clayton were certain that it was the deputy marshal, Orland Falk, who had put Clayton in jail.

'He's a long ways from us, too far to catch up,' an unperturbed Roop had decided. 'There's no need to do anything about him unless he gets in the way when we find Bailey.'

So they had ridden on, knowing that Orland Falk was behind, wondering what was in front of them. Now, with daylight fading fast, they were riding screened by dense brush on each side of the trail when Roop reined up.

'I can smell smoke,' he told them in a low voice.

'I can't,' Clayton said after sniffing the air, and Nancy silently agreed with him.

But Roop hadn't altered his mind. Dismounting, he told them to do the same. He spoke earnestly to them. 'Someone has made camp up ahead, and we'll have to skirt it. We walk, leading our horses. I'll go up front, then you, Nancy. You bring up the rear, Clay, and keep your ears skinned.'

They moved off slowly and quietly in an arc. Soon able to smell smoke, Nancy thought she was probably imagining it because Roop had said it was there. But then there was no doubt about it. There was smoke in the air, and as Roop signalled to them to be even more careful and quiet, the sound of muffled voices reached them.

After they had covered only a few more yards, Roop stopped and pointed through the thicket. Voices in animated conversation were clearer now, but it was impossible to decipher what was being said. Small flames leapt redly at the centre of a clearing. Nancy could then see men hunkering round the bright fire, drinking from mugs. Dramatically illuminated by the dancing tongues of flame, they were bearded ruffians, the kind of scum that had sunk too low to ever visit, let alone rejoin, civilized society.

Frightened by the sight of the men,

Nancy was relieved when Roop moved them forward once more. They walked their horses for what Nancy estimated to be from ten to fifteen minutes, before mounting up and riding for some miles. Roop halted them at a spot protected by the shoulder of a little knoll.

'This will suit for the night,' he said.

While Clayton and she unsaddled their horses, Nancy noticed that Roop had made no move towards doing the same with his mount. She was looking at him questioningly when he spoke.

'I'm going back.'

'What for?' a surprised Clayton asked, and Nancy waited anxiously for Roop's reply.

'That marshal of yours,' Roop said evenly. 'The fire will have died down by the time he gets there; he'll ride straight into that gang of cut throats.'

Nancy hoped that it was her concern for Roop that made her protest, but she had to admit that selfishness was mixed into it. 'Why risk your life for someone who is trailing your brother?'

'I couldn't let a man ride up on them all unsuspecting,' Roop told her before turning to Clayton. 'You hobble Nancy's horse and your own, Clay.'

'How can what you are going to do help, Roop?' Clayton argued reasonably. 'If they gun you down, Nancy and me are on our own; if you save Falk, then he'll cause us a heap of trouble.'

'I do things my way, Clay. Now get those horses hobbled. I'll be back before morning.'

As her husband knelt to do as he had been told, Nancy moved closer to Roop and begged him, 'Please, Roop, be careful.'

Looking deeply at her, Nancy hating herself for the way she was responding, when Roop spoke it was obvious to her that he had altered what he had originally intended to say. 'I'll take care, Nancy. I intend to find Bailey and put things right for you and Clayton.'

6

Orland Falk rarely ignored a danger signal that was produced by his reliable sixth sense. Whenever he had done so it had been to his cost, and it was no different on this occasion. Estimating that he had about one day in which to get closer to the Calmonts, he had decided to continue riding for half the night before taking a couple of hours' rest. In the next day or so the two men and one woman up ahead would reach Rosarita. Once there, with them amid El Toro and his bandits, even if the Calmonts did survive, which was unlikely, he would have problems rearresting Clayton Calmont.

The inner warning came as the trail ran through a dense thicket. Yet Falk couldn't envisage any danger up ahead because the Calmonts had passed through the area apparently unhindered. He carried on making good progress in the dark, and was congratulating himself on having made the right decision to ride on when it happened.

A rope had been stretched across the trail, with a man concealed in the brush at either side, each holding an end of the rope. As Falk rode up they lifted the rope over the horse's head so that it caught him across the chest. Jerked out of the saddle, Falk went backwards off his horse to crash to the ground.

Four men jumped on him as he lay stunned. Unable to resist, he felt his gunbelt swiftly unbuckled and snatched away. Lying there helpless, he could see another man helping himself to his rifle, while yet another claimed his horse by grabbing the reins. Regaining some feeling in his body, but still groggy, Falk was dragged to his feet and pushed into a clearing where other men waited around the glowing embers of a dying fire. They looked at him with interest, all seemingly eager for some sport with a captive.

Forced to sit down, he was sufficiently recovered to fight back, but any opportunity to do so was precluded by a man holding Falk's own rifle close to his head. It was plain that he had stumbled on one of the outlaw bands that roamed the hills. There were too many here for him to tackle, and he could tell they were desperate men who would kill him without compunction for his horse and the few possessions he carried.

With the muzzle of the rifle pressed against his temple, Falk made no move as one of the gang bent to relieve him of his money and the canvas poke it was kept in. Then the man searching him let out a whoop of delight as he found his marshal's badge and held it up so that the others could see the meagre light from the fire glint off it. They hooted and laughed derisively at him, delighted that they had captured a marshal. Falk knew that he could expect no mercy from them, and he cursed himself for stumbling on their camp like some novice lawman.

The hulking fellow who had found the badge pinned it to his own chest and paraded around to the laughter and applause of the others. Pointing at Falk, the man wearing his badge said mockingly, 'You are under arrest, *bandido*.'

All of them stood to form a menacing half circle round Falk. A gangly youngster with a thin, straggling beard giggled as he cried out, 'The Federal court is now in session.'

'I guess you'll act as judge, Aaron?' another said. Like the others, this renegade was in a dangerous state of half-drunkenness.

Aaron, who was obviously the leader of the group, took a step forwards. Falk looked up at a tall, heavy man with a short beard that jutted aggressively. There was an aura of power about him. His bearing suggested that he had once known better things, had lived a very different life. In an accepted society he would have made an imposing, distinguished figure. When he spoke his voice was a deep rumble.

'What is this man accused of?'

'Being a US marshal.'

'A serious offence, very serious,' the young member of the gang giggled.

'Indeed it is,' Aaron agreed, 'and I have no hesitation in finding the accused guilty.'

'And the sentence, Aaron?' the young thug asked, to continue the charade.

'His crime calls for the ultimate penalty,' Aaron intoned, his rich voice and solemnity causing him to sound like a real judge. 'The sentence is one of death.'

'Yippee!' the excitable young outlaw yelled. 'We're going to have ourselves a hanging.'

'No!'

It was the man holding the rifle to Falk's head who shouted the objection. 'I say we have a proper execution, the way the Mexes do it.'

There was not a hope of getting away. Sitting still, Falk, aware that he was going to die anyway, hoped that the man with the rifle would have his way. Death by musketry would be quicker and less painful than being hanged. With a vested, albeit final, interest in the outcome, he heard Aaron put the matter to the vote.

'We'll decide in the proper manner,' Aaron announced. 'Let's have a show. Who's in favour of a hanging?'

Only the gangling youngster and an elderly bandit raised their hands. When Aaron put the shooting option on offer, all the others voted for it enthusiastically.

'Right,' Aaron deliberated for a moment, hands behind his back, pacing up and down. 'Four of you form a firing squad. Kenny, you and Milhench tie him to that tree yonder. Keep him covered all the time, Toomey, these lawmen know a trick or two.'

Toomey kept Falk's rifle trained on him as Kenny, the gangling kid with the sparse beard, and a mean-looking man with deep-sunk eyes, pulled him to his feet and moved him a few yards to put his back against a tree.

A rope was thrown and Milhench caught it. As the bandit uncoiled the rope and shared it with Kenny ready to rope him to the tree, Orland Falk accepted that he had come to the end of the trail. Resigning himself to death, he deliberately sought a state of stupor to detach himself from the horror about to be inflicted upon him. Four bandits stood together a little way off, checking that their rifles were loaded.

'Keep your hands to your sides, Marshal,' Kenny grinned, blowing alcohol fumes on Falk as he came close to lay the rope across his chest.

Then, still grinning, Kenny began to collapse. It wasn't until the young outlaw hit the ground that Falk came to life and realized that a shot had come from out of the darkness. It had hit Kenny in the back, and the boy was dead.

In a state of panic, the other bandits were diving for cover as Falk heard his name called from the thicket. When he looked in the direction of the voice, it was to see a six-shooter spinning through the night, coming at him. As Falk plucked the gun from the air, so did a figure leap out of the brush to land in the centre of the circle, crouching with a gun in its hand. Falk immediately grasped the daring strategy his rescuer was employing. The outlaws had scattered to the perimeter of the circle, and now they couldn't fire at the intruder without the risk of hitting one of their own. Taking three quick strides to join the other man, Falk found himself looking at whom he guessed to be Roop Calmont.

Standing back to back, the two of them fired at every shadow, everything that made the slightest move. Falk saw Toomey step forwards, carrying his rifle but falling flat on his face to lie twitching in the throes of death. Another man screamed and threshed about wildly in the thicket. But both the element of surprise and the fear of shooting a comrade by accident had gone. The outlaws began to fling lead at Falk and Calmont.

Stepping apart to halve themselves as a target, they both dropped to one knee. A mistake made by an outlaw Falk recognized as Milhench, put him clearly on view in a break in the thicket. A faint moonlight outlined the outlaw against the sky behind him, making him an ideal target. With nowhere to go either to the left or the right, Milhench took the only chance he had by running at them fast to put himself safely between Falk and Calmont.

Quick as a flash, with the reflexes of a wild animal, Roop Calmont stood and tripped the running outlaw. A squeal of pain came from Milhench as he fell with his face touching the hot embers of the fire. Then he was screaming as Calmont put a foot on the back of his neck and pushed his face deep into the red-glowing wood. The screaming of the outlaw was a diversion that gave Falk the chance to bring down another two of the border ruffians.

Mercifully for him, Milhench died from suffocation and the agony of his burning face. Stepping away from him, Calmont fired at one of two men who were running for the horses. Hit in the back, the man threw up his arms, ran a few more steps, then crumpled to the ground. Falk let the second man mount up, then blew him out of the saddle with one sure shot.

Then it went quiet. The fire crackled as it gained new life to burn Milhench's head. The outlaws' horses moved restlessly, and then were still.

Falk spoke in a whisper to Calmont, 'Do you think that's all of them?'

'Not to my count,' Calmont replied. 'I make it one to go.'

'I didn't get the chance to do much counting,' Falk said ruefully.

Then they spun round together at a movement in the brush. A revolver was tossed out to land at their feet. The resonant voice of Aaron came from out of the darkness. 'There is my gun. I'm surrendering to you gentlemen.'

'Hold your hands out from your sides, and walk slowly,' Roop Calmont warned, keeping his gun aimed at the bulky figure of Aaron as it appeared.

Halting to stand facing them, Aaron said. 'As your prisoner, gentlemen, I shall expect humane treatment.'

'Sure,' Calmont said, keeping his .45 on Aaron as he added sarcastically, 'just like the fair treatment you were about to give the deputy marshal when I turned up.'

As Aaron cautiously moved a little closer, Falk was struck by something that was special about the man. Though his face was heavily fleshed there was still a handsomeness there. But it was his dark eyes, clearly visible up this close in the night, that were most compelling. They were impressive as he stared into Calmont's eyes and spoke without the slightest tremor in his deep voice.

'I take it that you are about to shoot me, sir,' Aaron said. 'Let me say that I am not afraid to die, but I would issue one warning.'

Giving his levelled .45 a significant little move, Roop Calmont said, 'It doesn't seem to me that you're in much of a position to give warnings, mister.'

'Ah, but you misunderstand, sir,' Aaron said, turning up the collar of his heavy coat as if suddenly noticing a chill in the night. Reaching up with his left hand, he took off his Stetson and held it against his breast like a mourner at a funeral. 'Do not make the mistake of regarding me as a commonplace mortal. You see, sir, my warning is not concerned with this world, but the next. Look deep into my eyes, for once you pull that trigger I will start to haunt you. Wherever you are, whatever you do, you will see — '

Orland Falk fired his gun then. His bullet hit Aaron in the chest. The big man took two short steps backwards before his legs gave way and he sank to the ground, dark eyes widening as they stared at Falk.

A puzzled Calmont looked at Falk, who bent over the body to lift Aaron's Stetson away to reveal that his hand held a small gun.

'A derringer, by God!' Roop Calmont gave a mystified shake of his head. 'I sure missed that one. A shoulder holster, I suppose.'

'Maybe, but he put the gun under his hat before giving himself up,' Falk answered, as he began to search among the bodies to retrieve his money, his badge and his rifle.

'I'm glad you spotted it, Falk,' Roop Calmont said, going on laconically, 'You sure must have mixed with some no-account *hombres* in your time.'

'Not until right now,' Falk said pointedly.

Roop Calmont chuckled heartily.

★   ★   ★

'Do you think I can improve on what I've done today, Pat?'

Sheriff Derek Decker waited anxiously for a reply from his deputy. They were riding back into Pine Notch after having spent an afternoon in a draw way out of town, where Shephard had supervised Decker's target shooting and fast-draw practice. This had been a twice-a-week ritual of late, with a dedicated Decker learning all the time. The deputy was good, real good, but now Decker considered himself to be drawing level, perhaps even surpassing, the gun skills of Pat Shephard. Decker was still smarting from having overheard old Matt Brown remark, 'That boy sheriff couldn't hit a barn door with a pesky cannon.'

Shephard's delay in answering irritated the sheriff, but didn't surprise him. A man of few words, his deputy was one of those brooding types who seemed to spend most of their time inwardly reliving or regretting their pasts. It hadn't ever sat well with

Decker that he had a subordinate who could handle a gun better than him. Though fairly easy-going generally, Decker couldn't bear either being second best or humiliated.

'I reckon you've reached your peak,' Pat Shephard said at last. 'You're as good as you're ever going to be.'

They started into West Street. Decker acknowledged Bennie Cault, who stood outside of his store enjoying the coolness of the late afternoon sun. A little further down the street Claude Sheen was proudly strolling with his pretty wife on his arm. They both turned into the Peak View Hotel before the sheriff and deputy reached them.

Seeing Ellie Sheen brought warm thoughts of Susan Staker to Decker's mind. New in town, Susan was training to take over as schoolma'am when Ellie had to leave to have her baby. Maybe it wouldn't be accurate to say that he and Susan were walking-out, but it was coming close. The pair of them got on real well. That was another reason, the most important one of all, for Derek Decker to prove himself.

'So, Pat, d'you think I'm good enough for what I've got to do?'

'I can't answer that, Sheriff, as I ain't got the faintest idea of what it is you've got to do.'

'Roop Calmont,' Derek Decker said bitterly. 'That man made a fool of me when he broke Clayton out of jail. The minute Roop puts one foot back in this town, Pat, I'm going to call him out.'

This had been festering inside Decker ever since the jail break. He didn't doubt that it had robbed him of the respect he once had from the townsfolk of Pine Notch when he was appointed their sheriff. Closer to home, he suspected that the pride his father had taken in him, after the years in which Decker had been all but disowned by his family, had begun to wane rapidly. All this, Decker was convinced, had been brought about by Roop Calmont.

'Well?' he asked sharply, needing his

deputy's opinion.

'Well, it's like this, Sheriff,' Shephard began slowly and thoughtfully. 'I was with the Doolin Gang when we hit the bank in South-west City, Missouri, and the whole town came out a-shooting at us. That was tough, Sheriff. A bullet went into Doolin's head and lodged inside his skull over the eye, and stayed there right up to his death. My horse was shot out from under me, and I ran for about two blocks, dodging lead all the way, until Tulsa Jack Blake, the Lord rest his brave soul, got me up on the back of his bronc. That was a mighty scary day, but if you gave me the choice of doing it all over again or facing Roop Calmont, I'd be on my way back to Missouri right this minute.'

This was a long speech for a man like Pat Shephard, and Decker knew that he should heed it. But Roop Calmont was increasingly becoming an obsession.

'I'm still going to do it, Pat. Are you saying I don't stand a chance against Calmont?'

'That's exactly what I'm saying, Sheriff.'

'Then I'm going to prove you wrong,' a determined Decker said.

'That ain't rightly fair,' Shephard said, 'because when I get to telling you I was right, you ain't going to be there to listen.'

* * *

They had ridden for three days together. Nancy and Clayton Calmont, both on edge since Roop had brought Orland Falk to join up with them, had barely spoken a word to the deputy marshal. Roop himself seemed to have a relaxed attitude towards Falk, but Nancy reasoned that he, unlike Clayton, had nothing to lose by having the lawman around. They were saddle weary, Nancy most of all, and Roop's attentive treatment of her had created a three-way tension with Clayton. Neither had she found it comfortable to be cool and distant with the deputy marshal, who was as friendly and polite as he had been when calling on them at the Double J. But he had been a threat to them then and was a bigger one now.

Roop hadn't said he had been in this area before, but Nancy suspected that he had a good knowledge of the San Jacinto hills. They climbed a steep slope now and came to a narrow pass that cut through what had to be the tallest hill. Coming out, they rode over a grassy knoll. Crossing this green space they began to descend a long slope of naked earth that was too steeply slanting and eroded for grass to gain a foothold. Small rocks and stones slid from beneath their horses' hoofs to go bouncing and clanking down into the valley below.

At the bottom they passed through arroyos and around patches of prickly pear until Nancy saw before them the first building since leaving the *cantina*. It was a sorry-looking, rickety log cabin with a sod roof.

'This is Mud Creek,' Roop

announced, betraying that he knew the place. 'The shack is an old hideout that will do nicely for what we want.'

What did they want? Nancy knew the basics, that they had to take Mitch Bailey back to Pine Notch alive, but how that was to be done, and who was to make the important decisions, she didn't know. All along she had assumed it would be Roop who took charge, but now she wondered what part Orland Falk would play, and whether the deputy marshal's presence would affect her husband's chances of being cleared of a crime he hadn't committed.

As the four of them sat in their saddles looking at the place, a rabbit revealed itself by coming out of the brush and stopping, hunched and apprehensive.

'There's our dinner,' Roop said quietly.

There was the crack of a shot and the rabbit flopped on to its side, dead. Startled by the noise, Nancy hadn't seen what happened, but she marvelled on realizing that Orland Falk had drawn, shot the rabbit and reholstered his gun at such a speed that neither Clayton nor she had witnessed the move.

'Go get it, Clayton,' Roop said, and his docile brother dismounted to obey the order.

Nancy cooked the rabbit, together with some wild vegetables Roop had walked a short distance to root from the ground, on a long-disused stove inside the cabin. Falk was carrying some coffee in his saddle-bags, and they enjoyed that with the meal.

They remained silent as they ate, each savouring the cooked food after a long spell of enforced fasting. When Orland Falk pushed his empty plate from him, he said, 'That was a handsome meal, Mrs Clayton, it reminded me of that real tasty pie you served up when I came to your ranch.'

The fact that the deputy marshal

remembered the pie, and the compliment he paid her made Nancy blush. An extra warmth came to her cheeks when she noticed that Roop was studying her reaction. Nancy suspected that he was enjoying her discomfort in a loving kind of way. She hadn't intended using the word 'loving' in her mind, and her cheeks burned even more hotly. It was becoming an increasingly awkward two-way pull for her between the Calmont brothers. Yet the involuntary excitement aroused in her by Roop in no way eroded her loyalty to Clayton. She would never permit it to do so.

'We're close to Rosarita now,' Roop explained, when he had finished eating. 'You and Clayton will stay here in the cabin with Falk, Nancy, while I go see if I can find Bailey in Rosarita.'

'Won't that be terribly dangerous?' Nancy, moved by fear for Roop, asked.

'From what I hear of it, El Toro has made that place into a fortress,' Falk commented. 'He'll likely have a stranger shot on sight, Calmont.'

'As a lawman, Falk,' Roop said with an easy laugh, 'you shouldn't overlook the fact that, with a slight change of circumstance, I would be the same as El Toro and those who ride with him. I'll be going to Rosarita as somebody on the run and wanting to join the Mexican's band.'

'You'll still be taking a huge risk, Calmont. If you're not back within three days I'm coming in after you,' Falk promised.

This made Roop chuckle. 'If I'm not back in three days I'm dead, *amigo*. Allow three days, yes, but then get Nancy and Clay out of here.'

With Clayton sitting beside her, Nancy didn't dare look at Roop. She was filled with admiration for a man who was more concerned about her own safety and that of his brother than he was his own.

'If Bailey is there,' Nancy began, 'how will you bring him out?'

'I'll decide that after I've seen how things are in Rosarita, Nancy.'

'What about Falk?' Clayton enquired. 'What about me?'

'You said back at Pine Notch that you have me for the rustling and Mitch Bailey was of no interest to you,' Clayton pointed out.

Making himself a cigarette, Falk didn't say a word until he had completed and lit it. Then he told Clayton, 'Things have changed since Pine Notch, Calmont. Back along the trail a'ways, your brother put his life on the line to save me.'

'We're even,' Roop protested. 'You saved my life by shooting that sidewinder Aaron.'

Hearing this made Nancy wonder what had transpired the night Roop had left her and Clayton alone. Roop must have done something really heroic to impress a veteran fighting man like the deputy marshal.

'That was easy, Calmont, It was you who took the chances, and I owe you,' Falk told Roop before speaking to Clayton again. 'I reckon I should repay him by saving your hide. If it's like you say it is, and Bailey rustled the IJ beef, then I'll do everything I can to help you.'

'Thanks,' Clayton said.

'It's your brother you have to thank,' Falk said. 'Riding into Rosarita isn't going to be fun.'

'There isn't time to thank me, Clay,' Roop said jokingly as he stretched and yawned. 'I want to get an early start, so I'm about to turn in.'

Watching Roop stand, pick up a blanket and stroll to a corner of the shack, Nancy couldn't believe how calm he was considering the perils he would be facing the next day.

7

Rosarita wasn't impressive. Yet though it was just a shambling collection of rude huts, it was the headquarters of El Toro, the Mexican bandit leader. As such it was impregnable. While still some miles away, Roop Calmont had been aware that every yard of progress he made had been scrutinized from ridges and hilltops. He had watched the signals pass between men on high, a message that said a stranger was riding in. When no more than a mile from the settlement, Calmont had been confronted by four Mexican horsemen led by a scar-faced man the others called Tagus. He had first been threatened, then, when he showed that he wouldn't be intimidated, questioned on why he was there, what he wanted in Rosarita.

'Only the foolish ride into El Toro's

territory,' Tagus had remarked.

'Also the desperate,' Roop had answered. 'They're to play cat's cradle with my neck back there, *amigo*. El Toro has to be a safer bet so far as I'm concerned.'

'Maybe so, maybe not, *muchacho*, but it is your neck not mine that you are risking,' the Mexican had said with a shrug, reining his horse about for Roop to follow him.

The other three horsemen went off to lie in wait for any more intruders. Just Roop and Tagus had ridden on into Rosarita. The people on the streets, something like an equal number of Mexicans and Americans, had a collective furtiveness, an invisible but still obvious mark of criminality about them. Yet despite the shanty-town buildings, there was an air of affluence about the place. A bellowing of cattle reached Roop Calmont's ears, and although Tagus deliberately took a circuitous route, he was able to glimpse huge pens as large as at any railhead at the end of a cattle trail. These pens were crammed full of rustled beef waiting to be moved out.

They passed some children playing in the street in the same skulking manner in which their outlaw parents behaved. Roop was taken down a side turning to one of the smaller huts. A heavily armed Mexican guard stood outside the door. He was a dark-skinned, menacing sentinel who eyed Calmont suspiciously even though he was with Tagus. Rosarita was a fortress, a sanctuary for law-breakers. It was home to desperate men with good reason to fear all strangers.

El Toro was alone inside the hut, sitting in a corner with a bottle of tequila in one hand and a glass in the other. He was small, but had the supple, snake-like physique of a man who could handle himself. As well as a gunbelt with a holstered six-gun, he wore a weighty bandolier and there was a Springfield rifle propped against the wall at his side. Incongruously, a large, ornate crucifix was affixed to the wall above his head.

Ignoring Calmont as he came in the door with Tagus, the bandit leader anxiously questioned his lieutenant: 'Any sign of Wellstead and his men, Tagus?'

'No, *jefe*,' Tagus answered. 'He must have been delayed.'

'No,' a worried El Toro shook his head. 'Something must have happened. When Aaron Wellstead says he'll be some place at a certain time, he's always there.'

Calmont smirked inwardly, pleased that he had knowledge that the Mexican lacked. Aaron Wellstead had to be the big man who had threatened to haunt him all his life. That had been a wasted threat, as it had been Orland Falk who had killed him.

'What have you brought me, Tagus?' El Toro asked, gesturing towards Calmont. His teeth were too large for him to completely close his mouth. This gave the impression that he was

157

constantly amused by what was going on around him. It was an illusion: the bandit leader was totally without a sense of humour. 'Is he some *bravo Americano* hoping to collect the twenty thousand dollars on the head of El Toro? Why you never bring an *Americano señorita* to brighten the nights of El Toro, *que*?'

'The American *señoritas* are cold, El Toro,' Tagus replied.

'New Mexico suns and a *caballero* like El Toro can warm their blood,' the bandit leader boasted with a flat, humourless laugh. 'Now, what are you going to tell me of this *hombre*?'

'He seeks to join us,' Tagus answered. 'The fame of El Toro has spread far and wide.'

Pouring tequila into his glass and drinking deeply, El Toro used the back of a hand to wipe his mouth, then pointed a finger at Calmont. 'Why you want to ride with us?'

'It's not healthy out there for me right now,' Calmont answered. 'But hiding away isn't a paying game. I figured that I could do myself a bit of good by joining you, El Toro.'

'Maybe I don't want you,' the Mexican muttered. 'I do not hire every damn *mal hombre* who comes uninvited to my headquarters. Should I know you?'

Calmont swiftly assessed the situation. El Toro wasn't the only infamous *hombre* around. He decided to give his proper name, expecting it to be known here, for his reputation to carry considerable weight in this lawless community. 'The name's Roop Calmont.'

'Never heard of you,' El Toro complained, waving a dismissive hand.

'I have heard the name, *jefe*,' Tagus said urgently. 'They speak of Roop Calmont as being very fast, very good with the gun, El Toro. This would be a good man to have with us. Especially for, you know . . .'

Understanding what his lieutenant had left unsaid, El Toro gave a satisfied,

'Ah,' before pointing a finger at Calmont again, enquiring, 'Where are you from, *amigo*?'

'Here and there, no place in particular.'

The bandit leader exclaimed with a mirthless laugh, 'Everyone here in Rosarita comes from no place in particular. *Madre di Dios*, maybe you come here to shoot El Toro in the back, how am I to know that isn't so?'

'I'm looking to hire my gun, not shoot you with it, El Toro.'

'The man holding the gun decides which way to point it, *amigo*.' El Toro shaped his right hand like a gun, forefinger extended. '*Un momento* the gun point that way, next *momento* I turn my back and the gun' — he twisted his hand so that his finger was pointing at himself — 'it points this way and, bang bang, El Toro, he is dead. Why should I trust you, heh? Why should I trust you, *Señor* Calmont?'

'Because I've rustled more head of beef than any man here in Rosarita,'

Roop bragged, 'and you need me real bad now that Aaron Wellstead isn't coming to help.'

'What you know about Wellstead?' The Mexican bandit was immediately suspicious.

'Only what I heard you and Tagus talking about, El Toro. Seems to me like you got a big job planned, but lack the wherewithal to get it done.'

Falling silent, El Toro took a long drink then dropped his chin to his chest in thought. There was a lengthy silence disturbed only by the steady thudding of the hoofs of a horse passing slowly outside. Roop waited patiently until the bandit chief was ready to raise his head and speak. 'I have much cattle here, *amigo*. El Toro has a fortune in beef ready to sell. It is not enough. A trail herd is heading toward the Black Range. With those longhorns added to what is already here in Rosarita, *muchacho*, El Toro can go home to Mexico, buy himself a big *hacienda* and many *señoritas*, and live forever happy.'

'Like I said, El Toro, you need me.'

'Maybe yes, maybe no, *amigo*. El Toro must remain here to look after things. I have a good man ready to ride out to the Black Range for me. If he says yes, Calmont, then that will be good enough for me, and I will hire you. Go fetch him, Tagus.'

El Toro didn't speak, but softly hummed a Mexican tune when he and Calmont were alone. Then Tagus returned with a shifty-eyed American of a type that Roop knew well and despised. They were outlaws made more dangerous by their treacherous nature. The bandit leader greeted the newcomer warmly.

'I have a good man here who wants to ride to the Black Range with you,' El Toro said, adding to Roop, 'Meet Mitch Bailey, *amigo*.'

Though he kept his elation hidden, Roop just couldn't believe this incredible stroke of luck. He had anticipated a long and hazardous search for Bailey in Rosarita, but the man had been delivered to him. Then the Mexican bandit spoke again to bring a sudden end to Roop's good luck.

'You probably know of this gun-slinger, Bailey,' the Mexican said. 'He is called Roop Calmont.'

Watching the frown crease Bailey's forehead, and his expression take on a wariness, Calmont cursed his foolishness in giving his real name to El Toro. Even though he and Clayton didn't look alike, the name was likely enough for Bailey to connect him with his brother.

Eyeing Calmont suspiciously, Bailey said in a way that was meaningful to the bandit leader, 'I ain't sure that we need another gun, El Toro.'

'Ah, *muy amigo*,' the Mexican addressed Roop, 'Mitch Bailey doesn't trust you, so why should I take a chance? Can you buy your way into El Toro's band, leave a bag of gold as security, and collect it when you return from the Black Range?'

'I have no gold,' Roop replied, but he was doing some quick thinking. Now that he had got this far in Rosarita, and Mitch Bailey was there before him, he didn't intend to give up. Necessity forced him to make an offer that involved his brother's wife. 'I heard your earlier wish for an *Americano señorita*, El Toro. I have my woman up in the hills. I could go get her tonight.'

The bandit leader showed an avid interest. 'Has she the fair hair, this *señorita*?'

'She's a redhead.'

'Ah,' El Toro licked his lips.

'I can have her here by morning,' Roop offered.

'You go get her, *muchacho*, and you can ride with Bailey to get those longhorns.'

'I want her back when I return, El Toro,' Roop warned to give his part of the deal authenticity.

This had the Mexican give a coarse laugh. 'After spending nights with El Toro, Calmont, your woman will not

164

want to go back to you. Bailey, take our *amigo* down to Pedro's place for some tequila before he rides out to fetch the redheaded *señorita* for me.'

Roop discovered that Pedro's place was a small and dirty shack. Pedro was fat, dirty and half asleep. Bailey and Roop drank together, leaning on a rough-wood counter. As Calmont had feared, Bailey had connected him with Clayton. While admitting that they were brothers, Roop convinced the other man that there was so much dislike between him and Clayton that they had not spoken for years. This had encouraged Bailey to boast of how he had sold the unsuspecting Clayton a ranch stocked with rustled cattle. Feigning a hearty laugh, Roop had given him a congratulatory slap on the back.

'I don't figure you, Calmont,' Bailey said now, as Roop refilled his glass for him. 'A man like you ain't got no need to work for El Toro.'

'I've never worked for any man,

Bailey, and I'm not going to start with El Toro.'

'I don't get what you're telling me.' Bailey shook a puzzled head.

'That herd at the Black Range, Bailey. You and me will ride down there, get shot at, eat dust all the way back, and what do we get for it? I'll tell you what, *pesetas* from El Toro. What would you prefer, my friend, to sit here in these hills with a couple of nickels, or live it up in an Austin honkytonk with a pocket full of rocks?'

With a short, harsh laugh, Bailey said, 'You must have a death wish, *compadre*. No one has crossed El Toro and lived.'

'We will,' Roop assured him. 'We rustle those longhorns and run them up to Texas. El Toro is a big man here, Bailey, but he sure isn't going to cross the border after us.'

The thoughtful expression on the face of the other encouraged Roop, but then Bailey shook his head. 'Can't be done, Calmont. There'll be at least a dozen of El Toro's *vaqueros* riding with us.'

'No.' Roop raised a hand to prevent Bailey from following up on this subject. 'I can get us enough hands out there. It'll be just you and me who leaves Rosarita, Bailey.'

'It won't work. We'd be cut down before we'd put a mile between us an' Rosarita,' Bailey said gloomily.

'Not the way I've got it planned. I'll see to it that El Toro is kept so busy that he won't even know we've gone until it's too late to catch up with us.'

'I reckon as how you've got me interested, Calmont,' Bailey nodded gravely, 'but there's one thing that bothers me.'

'What's that?'

'I ask myself why you need me in with you, and I can't come up with an answer,' Mitch Bailey worriedly replied.

'There's two answers to that,' Roop said with a false chuckle. 'First is that I owe a man who fixed my brother's flint the way you did.'

'I allow that the two of you ain't a bit alike,' Bailey commented. 'What's the second reason, Calmont?'

'Same thing, really. It took real brains to pull a trick like that, Bailey, and I'd sure appreciate having a man like you ride with me.'

Pleased by this, Bailey sort of mentally preened himself, then asked, 'You ain't really going to bring a woman in here for El Toro, are you, Calmont?'

'Oh, I'm bringing her to Rosarita, that's part of my plan,' Calmont answered. 'But she isn't going to be with that greaser long enough for him to get his hands on her.'

8

When Roop Calmont rode out of
Rosarita, the first stars were coming out
brightly over the northern peaks of the
San Jacinto hills. Feeling a westerly
wind mildly buffeting him, he fervently
hoped that it would prevail in the same
direction, and at similar strength, until
the following morning. That would
benefit greatly his still not fully
completed plan. At El Toro's headquarters his options had been limited to
either volunteering Nancy or abandon-
ing the campaign to take Mitch Bailey
back to Pine Notch. Roop knew what
her answer would have been could he
have asked her at the time. Even so, he
had taken a real liberty in volunteering
on her behalf. Aware that she wouldn't
hesitate for a moment, and that she
trusted him fully, he was also painfully
mindful that he could not guarantee her

safety. Assailed by an increasing misgiving, he suffered in the knowledge that he had no right to offer Nancy and his brother as potential sacrifices, for anything that happened to Nancy would affect Clayton terribly.

It had gone midnight when he arrived back at Mud Flats. The cabin was in darkness and, in the knowledge that Orland Falk would be alert and as instinctively savage as a wild animal at night, Roop reined up and mimicked the call of an owl, three times in quick succession.

Roop didn't hear the cabin door open, but he knew that it had, and that a rifle was now aimed in his direction. Falk's guarded call reached to him. 'Is that you, Roop?'

'It's me.'

'Then ride on in.'

Clayton and Nancy were astir when he dismounted and entered the cabin. Despite the late hour, Nancy rekindled the stove to produce a meal of rabbit stew for him, and make coffee for the others and herself. With her there it was the kind of homecoming that Roop Calmont had heard other men talk of, but had never experienced for himself. It gave him a feeling of contentment that he wanted to last, but knew was transitory. Unable to stop himself from covertly studying Nancy's pretty face, he didn't miss the trouble she took in making sure that their eyes didn't meet.

As Roop ate he gave an outline of the start of his plan, causing the usually placid Clayton to react animatedly. Pacing up and down in the cabin, his brother vehemently voiced his objections.

'I would rather be hanged ten times over for rustling, than put Nancy in danger.'

'She won't be in any danger with Roop there to look after her,' Falk contradicted him.

'Roop is only one man,' Clayton made a logical point, 'while Rosarita is full of outlaws.'

'I think we should hear all that Roop

171

has in mind,' Nancy said tentatively, not wanting to go against her husband, but frightened of losing the only chance to save him.

'I've heard enough,' Clayton snapped angrily.

'Well I haven't.' Orland Falk pointed a finger at Clayton, saying: 'You keep it shut for a while.' He made a go-on-talking gesture at Roop. 'You tell us all. Are you saying you can get Mitch Bailey out here?'

'Sure thing.' Roop gave a confident nod. 'He thinks me and him's going to be partners, but he'll learn different when he gets here.'

'You did well to win him over like that,' Falk complimented Roop.

'It wasn't hard,' Roop grinned. 'Like all his kind, Bailey's greedy. When I suggested we go the whole hog and double-cross El Toro, he was all for it once I showed him it would work.'

'Will it work?' Nancy asked respectfully as she poured them all more coffee.

'Roop Calmont's the man to make it work,' Falk said confidently. 'Tell us what you intend to do, Roop.'

Leaning back, stretching both arms above his head before relaxing, Roop began, 'Me'n Nancy ride in to Rosarita together, with El Toro thinking she's my woman and I'm giving him to her in exchange for joining his band — '

'You can stop right there, Roop,' Clayton cut in angrily.

'No, you stop it right there,' Falk told Clayton threateningly. 'You can have your say when everything that has to be said about capturing Mitch Bailey has been said, Clayton. Go on, Roop, let's hear the rest.'

'I've got it all doped out,' Roop recommenced. 'I leave Nancy with El Toro — '

When Clayton went to interrupt, Falk silenced him with a menacing glare.

'Then I'll start a brush fire to stampede the beef El Toro's holding in pens down there,' Roop went on. 'The cattle will take a trail across a coulee above El Toro's place, then they'll sweep through an arroyo to the left, heading east. While the Mex and his boys are chasing after them, we'll hightail it down the arroyo after the herd has gone through, and swing right to head west in this direction.'

'This will happen in darkness?' Clayton queried.

'No, during the day,' Roop answered, surprising both Nancy and Clayton, but going on to explain, 'Those who live outside of the law are ready for anything that happens at night. In daylight hours they relax and are not so alert.'

'It all sounds good to me,' Falk said. 'And Bailey will be riding with you?'

'At my side as a partner,' Roop made a laconic confirmation.

Calmer now, Clayton voiced his fears. 'I'm not saying I agree to any of this, but how would you get Nancy away from El Toro, Roop?'

'That Mex will lose interest in her

pronto, once his beef start to run. Brother,' Roop predicted, 'I'll have a fresh bronc saddled ready for her.'

'What if something should go wrong, like you get hit while lighting the fire or starting the stampede?' a still worried Clayton questioned.

'I don't have an answer to that, Clay,' Roop confessed.

'Then I'm not going to agree to Nancy going unless you let me ride with you to take care of her,' Clayton firmly stated.

Catching the makings Falk tossed to him after rolling a cigarette for himself, Roop's fingers deftly spread tobacco along paper, and he concentrated on this minor task as he spoke. 'That's a mighty poor idea, Clay.'

'I don't see that,' Clayton objected. 'Just because I'm not a gunslinger like you and Falk, doesn't mean that I won't fight to take care of my wife.'

'I don't doubt that you would, Clay, not for one minute,' Roop assured his brother. 'But from five miles out of

Rosarita there's a lookout atop every hill. They'll have been instructed by El Toro to allow me and a woman to ride in. If there's three of us, they'll blow you straight out of the saddle, Brother, and more likely than not finish us off, too. You wouldn't be taking care of Nancy, Clayton, but sentencing her to death.'

'That sure sounds like sense to me,' Falk said.

'It doesn't to me,' Clayton morosely announced. 'It's too risky, and I won't let Nancy do it.'

'It's the only chance we have of getting hold of Mitch Bailey to force him to testify to get you off the rustling charge, Clayton,' Falk cautioned. 'You don't need me to spell out the alternative, If we don't get Bailey, then I take you back to Pine Notch and hold you there so's you can stand trial before the judge.'

'Somehow I don't think Brother Roop would allow you to do that, Falk,' Clayton said with a hopeful look at his brother.

'In the circumstances,' Roop said with regret, 'I couldn't do anything other than let Falk take you in. Mitch Bailey is your only hope.'

'I'll get ready to ride out with you, Roop,' Nancy said in a quiet voice.

'I make the decisions, Nancy,' Clayton protested.

'Not this time you don't, Clayton,' Nancy countered, her voice even lower than before.

★ ★ ★

Having built up a tension in expectation of the return of Deputy US Marshal Orland Falk, with the Calmont brothers as captives, Pine Notch was wrong-footed by the arrival of Kansas Cal McCain. Though no Roop Calmont, the powerfully built McCain was a bully with a frightening reputation. Apparently wandering aimlessly through New Mexico, the argumentive McCain, who was wanted by the law, had begun a drinking session in Riley's saloon. It wasn't rare for the town to be visited by an outlaw, but they usually stayed just long enough to buy what they needed. McCain showed no sign of moving on. He was in a trouble-making mood that worsened as he consumed more liquor. He was on the prod, looking for a victim.

The first casualty was Carey Phillips. Just old enough to drink with the men, Carey had of late spent an hour or so a day exercising his long awaited maturity in Riley's place. In some innocent way he had fallen foul of Kansas Cal McCain, who had beaten the boy to a pulp. No one had tried to stop the big man, and Carey was now lying in the back room of Doc Petters' house, with even the old physician unprepared to predict whether or not he would survive the vicious attack.

Hearing of the unprovoked assault, Judge Jason Landseer, who was in town hoping for the return of the Calmont brothers, had sent to the sheriff's office requesting that action be taken. Arrest McCain without delay was the judge's message.

The problem was that Sheriff Derek Decker was out inspecting the site of an attempted stage hold-up, and Deputy Pat Shephard was at the Star Ranch investigating a botched attempt at rebranding cattle on the upper ranges. Pine Notch was temporarily without a law officer.

Something violent was about to happen in the town, that was certain. A silence gripped the place so tightly that it seemed to have squeezed out all the air so that West Street was oppressive. Fearless old Matt Brown paid regular and drink-prolonged visits to Riley's to keep an eye on Kansas Cal and report back to the townsfolk, who were agog. The general feeling was that it would be better for everyone concerned, though not Cal McCain, if Shephard arrived back in town before his boss, Decker. In the always candid words of Matt Brown, this was 'a man's job that couldn't be done by a boy, in particular a half-baked kid like Decker.'

The only one in town who didn't agree with this was Paul Landor, the obese writer, and his motives were entirely selfish. Lander saw less profit in a story telling how Pat Shephard had killed a half-drunken McCain, than in a juicy printed tale of how McCain had taken Sheriff Decker apart, piece by piece.

With the passing of time, most Pine Notch people had taken a liking to Sheriff Decker, and they didn't want a brute such as McCain let loose on him. Possibly the most anxious person in town was the delectable Susan Staker, who stood beside Ellie Sheen outside the schoolhouse, looking up West Street, willing Decker, who had become her suitor, not to ride back in before his deputy.

The broad and dusty street was as lonesome as a tomb. Even Bonzo,

Bennie Cault's skinny brown cur, was acting in a sneakily strange way. Either because the afternoon sun was hotter than usual, or due to some canine gift of prophesy, Bonzo had forsaken the usual damp, shady spot beside the well next to the store to crawl a long way in under the sidewalk to where flying bullets wouldn't reach.

An inaudible sigh swept the full length of West Street as Derek Decker rode in from the north end. Horse moving at a leisurely pace, the sheriff glanced towards his office, but then gazed longingly into the middle distance to where Susan Staker stood. Decker was too far away to detect the anxiety that was torturing the girl. He was, in fact, totally unaware of any problem until Matt Brown came hurrying up to report Cal McCain's presence in town.

Nodding gravely as he listened to the news, the young sheriff gave his gunbelt what could have been a nervous hitch, then started to walk slowly towards

Riley's saloon. Bennie Cault and Claude Sheen walked up to stop him.

'McCain's a dangerous man, Decker,' Cault advised. 'Best if you wait for Pat Shephard to get back.'

'I can handle McCain,' Decker replied, moving past Cault.

Sheen spoke diplomatically. 'Nobody's saying that you can't handle McCain, Sheriff, but Pine Notch needs both you and your deputy. Please wait until Shephard is here to go to the saloon with you.'

Not answering, Decker moved round the two men and walked resolutely down the street. Appearing not to have seen Susan running in his direction, he strode in through the door of the saloon.

McCain, a big, broad-shouldered man of forty, with a black moustache shaped like a horseshoe, both ends dropping well below his chin, turned his head as he stood by the bar. Sleepy-eyed, he took a look at Decker then turned his head to where old Matt

Brown and some other Pine Notch men huddled together as if for protection.

'What have we here, folks?' McCain mockingly enquired. 'It sure looks like a bird, but I don't see no tail feathers sticking out on it. Does it bite?'

Step not faltering, Decker walked up to McCain, who was more than twice his size, saying, 'You're under arrest, McCain.'

'It has to have escaped from a circus!' McCain turned laughingly to the townsmen.

'I'm Sheriff Decker, McCain,' Decker said, tapping the star pinned to his chest to add emphasis. 'Like I said, you're under arrest.'

'You're beginning to irritate me, kid,' McCain became angry. 'Let me tell you the three choices you've got: you can turn around and walk out of here, or I'll take you by the seat of your pants and the nape of your neck and throw you out.'

'You can't count, McCain,' Decker grinned, while the watching men cringed. 'That was two choices.'

'The third choice, you undersized monkey,' McCain hissed out his words, 'is for me to kill you right here and now.'

'That's the choice I'll go for,' Decker said with an easy smile.

'You little runt,' McCain raged, his powerful shoulders hunching forward, his head drawn down, and his dark eyes just two tiny slits in his sweating face, as he threw out a huge fist.

The punch may well have torn Decker's head from his shoulders, but he bobbed underneath it, weaved to confuse McCain who was ready to throw another punch, then stepped in close to deliver left and right-hand punches in quick succession. Cracking like pistol shots, Decker's left fist landed jarringly against McCain's jaw, while the knuckles of his right hand exploded against the big man's mouth, mashing the lips and doubling the size of the moustache with blood that ran from both ends.

As strong as a full-grown bull, McCain fell back only half a step before lunging forward on the attack once more. Mouth leaking blood fast, his right fist grazed against the side of Decker's head with enough force to send the sheriff staggering. But then Decker took the initiative again. Too blindingly fast for McCain, he slammed another left hand to the jaw, and when his right fist drove hard into the damaged mouth for the second time, McCain roared like a maniac as he went backwards, smashing a table to pieces as he crashed to the floor.

Looking down at the fallen man for a moment, a satisfied Derek Decker turned away, massaging his right knuckles with his left hand. It was Matt Brown who yelled a warning as McCain raised himself up on one elbow.

'Look out, Decker,' Brown cried. 'Watch his gun hand. He's quicker than all get out on the draw!'

It seemed that Decker hadn't heard. Matt Brown and the others shrank back against the wall of the saloon as Kansas Cal McCain's six-gun cleared leather. It looked like the end of the sheriff, but Decker swung round, drawing his gun and firing all in one practised movement.

McCain didn't get the chance to pull the trigger of his gun. He died instantly from Decker's bullet, which had gone in downwards at the hairline.

'I'll send someone over for the body,' a cool and composed Decker told Riley, who was standing behind his bar, immobile with shock.

Pat Shephard had pushed in through the crowd by the door, a crowd that had Susan Staker as a member, an expression of hero worship on her face. As Decker came towards him the deputy grinned and paid his young boss a compliment. 'That was a mighty fine piece of shooting, Sheriff.'

'I guess that I'm ready for Roop Calmont now,' Decker said with a pleased smile.

'Now I wouldn't go so far as to say that,' Shephard cautioned hastily.

★ ★ ★

Nancy and Roop rode together unspeaking. But she was aware, and sensed that he also recognized, some indefinable communication going on between them. They shared a romantic closeness, so profound that they could have been a couple riding out of the first dawn of civilization. That description fitted perfectly, but it didn't strike Nancy as her kind of thinking. Perhaps she had read it long ago in a now-forgotten book.

Whatever it was, she knew she had to stop it. In the final analysis the security offered by her husband was far more valuable than the excitement that drew her to his brother. The hidden depths to Roop frightened her.

Since they had left the cabin at Mud Flats he had ridden with an assurance that said he knew every canyon, ridge, hog-back, divide; every spider-webbed trail of this rock-bound fastness.

A yet-to-be-visible sun had lightened the sky so that as they reached a rocky point about which the trail and a creek bent, the yellow-brown natural ramparts of Rosarita were visible up ahead. It was a sight that awakened Nancy's first real fear about what was to happen.

With the hoofs of their horses making no sound on thick turf as they passed through cottonwoods and willows, she was startled when Roop reined up. Pushing his Stetson back on his head, he looked at her intensely.

Uncomfortable under his scrutiny, she lowered her head. Fearing what he might say, but at the same time wanting to hear it, she waited. When he did speak it was with an uncharacteristic reticence.

'I'm not used to this kind of thing, Nancy. Seems to me that if the right words are there somewhere, I just can't find them.'

'They are words best left unsaid, Roop,' she said quietly. 'Anyway, I think I know what you want to say.'

'Maybe for us the knowing is enough?' he questioned.

'For us it has to be,' Nancy replied.

'I guess so,' Roop said unhappily, reining his horse about to continue on the trail to Rosarita.

Soon they were riding between lowly buildings and being eyed suspiciously from all sides. As they arrived outside of El Toro's hut, the Mexican stepped out, smiling with too many teeth, pulling off his sombrero to sweep it low in one hand as he bowed to Nancy.

'Welcome to my humble abode, señorita,' he said as he helped her dismount. 'You are a queen whose beauty turns my home into a palace.'

Trying to smile, Nancy heard the

bandit leader dismiss Roop with a curt *gracias*. As Roop pulled his horse round to head to where Mitch Bailey stood waiting for him, she felt more alone than ever before in her life.

9

Everything went to plan after Roop had, reluctantly, left Nancy with El Toro. What had been little more than a slight breeze when they had ridden in, was now a strengthening wind that suited his purpose ideally. Coming from the west it would speed the fire behind the cattle to keep them moving. Unseen, Roop had taken a saddled horse and concealed it ready for Nancy in the grove of alamos at the back of the bandit leader's hut. He had left his own mount saddled and hidden a hundred yards from El Toro's hide-out.

Though a niggling worry over Nancy occasionally distracted him from his task, Roop was not overly concerned for her. El Toro was fond of boasting that he had never loved a woman who had not given herself freely to him. Whether or not that was true Roop didn't know, but it meant that the Mexican would spend considerable time wining and dining Nancy. Before the Mexican bandit got round to being serious, Roop would have the stampede in progress and would be back for her.

His biggest problem that morning, the weakest link in the chain of his planning, was Mitch Bailey. Bailey's terror of El Toro had enlarged to proportions that made him a risk to Roop. If something should panic Bailey, then it was possible that he might attempt to curry favour with the bandit leader by betraying Roop. To prevent this happening, Roop had sent Bailey out to wait at a point safely away from the path of the intended stampede, and where Roop could collect him when he rode out with Nancy.

As the flames crackled and smoke rose, too far from the buildings to be spotted as yet, the cattle in the pens were disturbed. Bellowing, they began to crash about. At first restricted by space, they were soon crashing against each other as fear took hold.

Content that the fire had gained enough strength to continue, Roop took a tortuous route back towards the buildings. Moving slowly and carefully to avoid being seen, he was quite a way from El Toro's headquarters when the wind gained force to fan the fire into a sudden conflagration. Fierce red tongues of fire reached high into the air. As Roop had planned, the westerly wind guided the flames and smoke in an arc behind the cattle. Panicking men were running and shouting, but then their voices were drowned out by the bellowing of a mighty herd on the move. The sound of the wooden pens cracking up under the mass weight of frightened cattle came as an irregular number of explosions.

Men were on horseback now, riding off to attempt the impossibility of controlling the stampeding cattle. Roop heard a series of shots as a try was made at bringing down the lead cows in the hope of turning back the herd. With the fire now an inferno, Roop knew that this was an exercise doomed to failure. The ground was literally shaking as thousands of pounding hoofs made a constant, thunderous roar.

Stealthily entering an alleyway between a dilapidated hay barn and a bunkhouse of sorts, Roop was heading for where he had left his own horse, when someone holding a rifle entered the alley from the other end. It was the scar-faced Tagus, who, on recognizing Roop, spoke urgently.

'*Madre di Dios*, Calmont, the whole world is on fire. Get your horse. We need every man we can if we're not going to lose those longhorns.'

Roop took too long to think of a way out of this predicament, puzzling Tagus. Then the puzzlement of El Toro's lieutenant became suspicion before turning into a rage that brought his rifle up to cover Roop.

'You!' Tagus gasped. 'It was you who started the fire! Why?'

Roop's answer was an upward kick

with his right foot. The toe of his boot caught the barrel of the rifle. Tagus pulled the trigger but the bullet went past the side of Roop's head, close but not perilously so.

Before Tagus had an opportunity to bring the rifle down and try again, Roop grabbed it with both hands. Wresting the weapon from the Mexican's grasp and placing it horizontally across his throat, Roop slammed Tagus back against the wall, slowly throttling him until the Mexican brought his knee up hard into Roop's groin.

Dropping the rifle, Roop doubled over in agony. Tagus, who was living up to his tough, scarred looks, proved to be an able fighter, using his knee yet again, this time to Roop's face, sending him crashing backwards.

Off balance, Roop fell awkwardly to the ground. He saw Tagus coming at him, and realized that he had quite a fight on his hands. Most worrying of all was the fact that Nancy would be waiting for him. If El Toro hadn't left his hide-out to take charge of the men trying to gain control over his stamped-ing cattle, then every minute that Roop was delayed here was putting Nancy in greater peril.

On his knees, looking up at the advancing Tagus, Roop saw a pall of black smoke filling the sky. He could smell fire, taste it so clearly that it had to be that the direction of the wind had changed. This could cause considerable problems. It meant that he had to finish Tagus off quickly.

Having picked up his rifle, the Mexican used it in close-quarter combat by swinging the stock at the kneeling Roop's head. Partially evading the blow by swaying to one side, Roop winced as the butt of the weapon caught him a glancing but painful blow on the temple. Purposely falling forwards, Roop wrapped both arms around Tagus's legs at knee height. Holding on tight and throwing himself backwards, Roop pulled the Mexican off balance. As Tagus landed on top of Roop, the rifle fell from his hands.

Rolling out from under the Mexican, Roop grabbed the rifle and twisted onto his back so as to aim it. Although he now had the advantage, it was lessened by the lithe Tagus coming quickly up onto his feet to aim a kick at Roop.

Seeing the boot coming his way fast, Roop, lying flat on his back, had no way of avoiding it. Pointing the rifle upwards, he pulled the trigger and hoped.

The slug went in under Tagus's chin. Roop watched as it travelled upwards to blow off the top of the Mexican's head, tearing most of his face away in the process. That was the last Roop saw before the kick aimed by the already dead Tagus caught him heavily on the side of the head.

When Roop opened his eyes he had to blink several times to relieve a stinging brought on by smoke. The body of Tagus lay across his legs, and he had to push it off before getting groggily to his feet. With nothing to indicate how much time had passed while he had been unconscious, Roop hoped that the sound of thundering hoofs and the cries of excited men meant that it hadn't been long. Yet he was frantic with worry over Nancy.

Running to his horse, there no longer being any need for caution, he leapt up into the saddle. Rowelling his bronc's flanks cruelly, he galloped it back through the alleyway, unavoidably smashing Tagus's body with its hoofs, then swept into the street leading down to El Toro's hut.

Smoke hung like a thick fog, proof enough of a change in wind direction. Peering through it as he rode, Roop saw movement outside the bandit leader's hut. At first unable to make out what it was, he cursed to himself as he rode closer. El Toro was on a huge black stallion, spurring it away from his hut. Screwing up his eyes to peer through the reeking haze, Roop had his suspicions confirmed: the Mexican bandit was holding Nancy across his saddlehorn.

Roop couldn't risk a shot, but he galloped after the big black horse into thickening smoke that blurred everything. Within minutes they were riding beside a heaving, unstoppable sea of cattle. The longhorns shouldn't be running here. All of Roop's plans had been ruined by the change in the wind. He couldn't be sure, but felt it possible that Mitch Bailey would be directly in the path of the fast-running herd.

But saving Nancy took priority now. El Toro was riding dangerously close to the stampede. It wasn't likely that the experienced bandit-leader's thinking had been affected by what was happening. Doubtless he knew that Roop was in pursuit, and his strategy was to force his pursuer to concentrate more on the stampeding cattle than on him.

Through the smoke, Roop could see daring riders hopelessly trying to stem the massive, heaving flow of longhorns. Some were paying with their lives. In the turmoil, above the concerted, earth-shaking thud of countless hoofs, rose the screams of riders and the louder, more harrowing shrieks of horses as men and beasts went down under the flaying hoofs of cattle.

Drawing up abreast of El Toro's horse, Roop was close enough to see the wild-eyed look on Nancy's face as she recognized him. El Toro drew his pearl-handled revolver and blazed away at Roop. But scoring a hit would have been a fluke at that speed and in those conditions. The dust kicked up by the cattle had thickened the smoke. When his gun had been emptied, El Toro, as if something told him he would have no further use for it, let it fall from his fingers. Roop could tell that Nancy was yelling something at him, but there was no chance of hearing what it was.

Keeping pace with the bandit and his captive, Roop uncoiled his lariat and slipped one end over the horn of his high-peaked Mexican saddle. Getting his timing right, he stretched his right hand out. The riata snaked out, the loop pausing above El Toro's head before dropping as if guided by something magical.

But the experienced bandit leader was alert to all that was happening. It looked as if Roop's idea of roping him out of the saddle was assured of success, but at the last second El Toro performed a bob of his head and a sideways shrug of his shoulders and the lasso slid clear of his body.

Prepared to pull in the rope and try again, Roop watched helplessly as he saw the noose drop over the horns of one of the stampeding cattle. As the rope went taut, his horse, which as far as Roop knew had never been used by a cowpuncher, decided to take the strain like a well-trained cow pony. The noose ran tight. There was no way in which Roop's bronc could even check the longhorn's headlong flight. It was all happening fast, but Roop felt his horse being pulled towards the stampeding herd. The bronc was struggling gamely, but the outcome was inevitable. Both Roop and his mount were going to end up trampled by the longhorns.

With his horse tilting alarmingly to the left under the pull of the rope, Roop felt for the knife at his waist with fumbling fingers. Locating the handle, he pulled it from the sheath and slashed at the stretched-tight rope. His first hacking cut severed about half the strands, the next all but severed the rope, but it took a third swing with the knife to free him and his horse.

It was too late. The bronc had been pulled over past the point of no return. Just before it crashed in the dust on its left side, Roop pulled his foot out of the stirrup and lifted his leg clear. He was thrown wide, choking on dust as longhorn hoofs slammed into the ground so close that he expected them to slash him to pieces at any moment. Rolling to his right through the dust, he got up onto his feet just as his horse was doing the same. Roop was reaching for the reins when the shoulder of a running steer hit him full in the back, and the tip of one of its horns tore his shirt away from his shoulder.

The impact smashed him face first against the side of his horse, panicking the animal so that it raced away. With the reins yanked from his hand, the badly winded Roop reached up to grab the saddlehorn with both hands. For a while he was pulled along by his frightened bronc, his toes dragging through the dust. Smoke and dust prevented him from seeing further than a few yards. Nancy and El Toro had to be well up ahead by now. Dispirited, unable to reach for the reins, Roop just clung on.

But his horse had instinctively pulled away from the stampede, saving itself and Roop. Encouraged by this, Roop pulled himself back into action. At first moving his feet in an inadequate run, he then kept his grip on the saddle and took bounding little leaps beside his horse in the style of a trick rider. When he had his jumps synchronized with the pace of his horse, Roop sprang up from the ground straight into the saddle. Holding the bronc's neck with one hand, he leaned forward to recover the reins with the other.

Back in control of his horse, he spurred it. Too frightened to realize it should be exhausted, the bronc broke into a gallop. With the smoke clearing a little up ahead, and assuming that El Toro was maintaining his tactic of riding close to the longhorns, Roop reined his horse to the left. The memory of the out-of-control herd made the bronc resist for a moment, but then it obeyed.

With the thunder of hoofs loud in his ears once more, an elated Roop saw that he was closing on El Toro. Even as fine a horse as the big black stallion was slowed by carrying two people, despite Nancy being of slight build. The bandit looked over his shoulder to stare into Roop's eyes before turning to keep control of his horse. With no lariat to use for a second try, Roop drew abreast of the stallion once more. He wasn't sure if Nancy knew he was there this time. She was suffering badly from the rough ride.

Roop had to take a chance. Freeing his right foot from the stirrup, he kicked out. The sole of Roop's boot hit El Toro in the side with such force that the bandit went sideways off his horse. El Toro knew that all was lost, but he consoled himself by pulling Nancy with him.

This was what Roop had feared. Keeping his bronc tight against the stallion, he reached over to the far side of El Toro's horse to clutch at Nancy. His fingers found her belt and hung on. Reaching with both hands to Roop's arm, she began to slowly pull herself up. The bandit was clinging desperately to her skirt, but the motion of his horse as it banged against him was dislodging El Toro.

A hard man to the end, the Mexican didn't make one sound as he fell among the longhorns. Roop had respect for El

Toro as he saw him first jostled by the cattle, then kicked as he fell among their legs, before being mashed under their hoofs. The bandit's death was silent and heroic.

But Roop had his own problems. The out-of-time jolting of his horse and the stallion was making it difficult for Nancy to cling to him. The two animals were parting so that the strain on Nancy's clawing fingers was too strong. Knowing that she was about to let go, Roop held the reins of his own galloping bronc tight in his right hand, clasped the saddlehorn of the stallion with his left hand, and transferred mounts. Once in the saddle on the stallion he used his left arm to pull Nancy up in front of him. With his guidance she moved back into the saddle as he edged out of it.

Once Nancy was in the saddle and holding the reins of the stallion, Roop pulled his own horse close and threw himself across. Missing the saddle he lay across the bronc's rump on his stomach, being bounced up and down, his legs kicking uselessly in the air. Then he felt Nancy's hand gripping his ankle and pulling and pushing so that his body turned and he was at last able to get a grip on his horse.

Safely back in the saddle, Roop reached out a hand in thanks to Nancy, and she clutched it briefly. They slowed a little, wanting to let the herd get clear, before following in its wake.

Then they were both bringing their horses to a skidding halt as an unbelievably horrific sight faced them. Another change in wind direction was bringing the fire up the arroyo towards them. There was a stench of burning flesh and singeing hide as the long-horns, unable to stop, ran straight into a wall of leaping orange flames.

So fast was the fire moving that tongues of flame licked out dangerously close to them, the heat too near for comfort. Signalling to Nancy, Roop swung his horse to the west and she did the same with the stallion. They headed off, away from where longhorns were rushing to die as unwilling sacrifices.

Within minutes they knew the worst. The wind was carrying the fire round in a half-circle that was cutting off every avenue of escape, trapping them.

'We are done for, Roop,' Nancy said sorrowfully, between hacking coughs brought on by the smoke.

'Not yet,' he said, silently agreeing that she was right, but not wanting her to know that.

Everything now seemed pointless. If the wind hadn't ruined his plans and he and Nancy had got away, they would be back where they started regarding his brother and the ranch. There was no chance that Mitch Bailey had survived the raging inferno that Roop's arson scheme had become.

Followed by billows of smoke and an intensifying heat, they went slowly down a grey slope strewn with boulders. Looking back, Roop saw the juniper trees that had dotted their way being reached for hungrily by the fire.

They passed through cottonwoods and willows to come upon a murmuring brook that was too narrow to protect them from the fire, but was capable of cooling them.

Dismounting, they scooped up the water with both hands and splashed it on themselves. It stung their faces, which they hadn't realized had been slightly scorched. Looking up, they saw a ring of flames and smoke all around them, moving ever inwards as if the fire had a mind of its own and intended to engulf them.

'I have an idea, Nancy,' Roop said, his voice hoarse.

'It won't save us, will it, Roop?'

'I doubt it,' he answered honestly. 'Probably all it will mean is dying out there somewhere instead of dying here.'

With a rueful, brave, little grin, Nancy said, 'Let's give it a try. There's something cowardly about standing here and letting it close in on us.'

Moving fast, Roop loosened the cinches on his bronc first, and then the stallion, pulling the saddle-blankets out from underneath before tightening up the leather straps again. Going to the brook, he dropped both blankets in and let them soak until they could absorb no more water. Then he pulled them out, heavy and dripping, and told Nancy to mount up.

When she was in the saddle, he threw one soaking-wet blanket up to cover her. Then he got up into the saddle and pulled the other blanket over himself. Making a monk-like cowl, he called to her to do the same.

'Ready?' he asked.

'Ready,' Nancy confirmed, 'but I'm not sure what for.'

'We ride west,' he said, pointing toward what looked like a high cliff of flame. 'Straight into that.'

This time it was Nancy who reached a hand out to him. They touched fingers briefly, then rowelled their mounts at a gallop towards the fire. The horses screamed, trying to stop, but Nancy and Roop dug in their spurs unmercifully. They had to fight the animals hard to keep them facing straight ahead when they wanted to veer to the left or right to avoid the fire.

Then they were in it, flames crackling all round them, smoke chokingly thick. But they kept going, protected in the beginning by the cold of the water in the blankets. But as they went further and further into the fire, with no sign of it letting up, the blankets quickly dried and were beginning to be scorched by the flames. The heat became unbearable and their chests felt as if they were about to explode because they couldn't breathe.

Swaying in the saddle, Nancy's head dropped to her chest and she dropped her reins. Under no pressure now, the frightened stallion stood still. Wheeling his horse about, his right boot on fire, his blanket alight at the edges, Roop reached down and caught the stallion's reins. Having to battle both horses now, he pulled the stallion along behind him, turning regularly to look with sore eyes to see that the barely conscious Nancy was still in the saddle.

When his own horse, singed, terrified and totally spent, came to a halt, Roop Calmont was ready to give up. Lungs full of smoke, he coughed and retched, as he could hear Nancy doing close behind him. Having given it his all, he slumped in the saddle, beaten.

But a sudden gust of wind swept away the smoke in front of him. Convinced that he was having a near-death hallucination, Roop could see green trees and a blue sky up ahead. His horse must have shared the vision, for when he gave a gentle kick with his heels, the faithful bronc moved.

Then they were clear of the smoke and breathing fresh air in great gulps. Throwing off his own smouldering blanket, Roop, still coughing, dis-mounted and pulled the blanket from Nancy. Recovering as he took her down from the saddle, she temporarily stifled her coughing to smile her relief.

Standing together, with Roop supporting Nancy in his arms, they controlled their breathing so as to exchange smoke for air with as less trauma for themselves as possible. Glancing around as the soreness cleared from his eyes, Roop was startled to see a forlorn-looking bay horse standing some twenty yards from them. At sight of the animal, Roop scanned the area. He saw what appeared to be a body sprawled on a hummock, partly obscured by giant cacti.

Lowering Nancy to the ground in a sitting position, he hurried over to find a collection of charred clothes and skin. The face was blackened but otherwise unscathed. Disbelief was Roop's first reaction as he recognized the burnt man.

'It's Mitch Bailey,' he called to Nancy.

'Is he alive, Roop?'

Making a quick check, Roop reported, 'Yes, but only just.'

10

With the buildings of Pine Notch in
view, tantalizingly close, they had to
stop at the top of a rise. Mitch Bailey,
most of his body terribly burnt, was
close to death. His condition had
made their ride from Mud Flats
frustratingly slow, and now fear of
losing this vital witness made them
stop yet again. The three men eased
Bailey down from the saddle with
immense sympathy and consideration,
yet they couldn't avoid exacerbating
his agony. They laid him on the grass,
his body stiff and dry, as Nancy knelt
to hold a bottle so that water trickled
into his mouth. Then she tenderly
bathed his face. Bailey opened his
eyes, but she couldn't tell whether or
not he could see her.

Looking down at the town, Orland
Falk spoke for all of them when he said,

'It would be real bad to lose him now we're so near.'

The situation put Nancy on edge. On the occasions that they had let Bailey rest he'd regained enough strength to speak. Knowing that he was going to die he had stated his willingness to swear that he had duped Clayton. Each time this had occurred Nancy had wondered why Orland Falk, as a deputy marshal, hadn't acted in some way on what Bailey had said. This would have made certain that Clayton would be absolved once they were back in Pine Notch. The way things were, Bailey might well die without uttering another word. Now that they were so near, and yet so far from putting the whole thing right, she could restrain herself no longer.

'Couldn't you write down what Bailey has said, Marshal Falk?' she asked.

'I can write it down, ma'am, but it would have no standing in a court of law unless he signs it,' Falk replied, reaching for Bailey's red-raw hand, where the only skin not burned off had formed flapping, pus-seeping blisters. He held it up. 'He's not going to sign anything with this hand.'

Spirits sinking, she said miserably, 'Then we can't do anything even when we're back in town?'

'I hope the judge will be there,' Falk said. 'He can hear what Bailey has to say, and that will be good enough for any court.'

'If Bailey can still speak when we get him there,' Roop qualified the situation.

'If he's alive when we get him there,' Clayton unhappily added.

'He's lasted this long, he's just got to hold on,' a wishful Nancy said.

'Where's the doctor's place in town?' Roop enquired.

'This end,' Nancy replied. 'Just opposite the schoolhouse.'

'Good, then there's no point in hanging on here. We have to gamble on him staying alive without resting any longer.'

Tacitly agreeing with Roop, Falk and Clayton lifted Bailey gently from the ground and up on his horse. A low moan escaped from the dying man. Recognizing the sound as a signal of acute suffering, Nancy felt callously selfish in welcoming it as reassurance that Bailey was still alive.

Putting a hand lightly on Roop's arm, she moved him away from the others. It might look suspicious to Clayton, but she needed to speak to Roop. Once they were in town the opportunity would be lost, most probably forever.

'I want to thank you for everything that you've done, Roop,' she said quietly.

'No need,' he shrugged, adding seriously, 'You said that we shouldn't speak of our feelings, Nancy, but you understand how it is?'

'I understand how it is,' she answered, 'but what is most important is that we both understand how it *must* be.'

217

'There's no question about that. Clay is my brother.'

'God bless you, Roop,' she whispered, as she saw the others were ready to move on.

Making a slow and unnoticed entrance into town, the little procession stopped outside of Doc Petters' house. The old physician, a fussy little man, answered the door and ushered them in. Clayton and Roop carried Bailey in and laid him on a bed next to Carey Phillips, whose black-and-blue face was swollen to something like twice its size. A sad Nancy looked at the boy, then turned her attention to the doctor, who had begun to work on Bailey.

'There's no chance of saving this man,' Dr Petters pronounced.

'We know that, Doc,' Roop said. 'What we need is to keep him going until we can get a judge here. How long has he got?'

'Only a very short time, but you're in

luck. Judge Landseer is staying up at Claude Sheen's place,' Petters said.

Roop was going out of the door when Falk called him back. 'I'll go fetch the judge, Roop. You forget the last time you were in Pine Notch you broke the jail open.'

'I'm trying to forget an awful lot of things,' Roop said reflectively.

The doctor went to a sink and began carefully mixing a potion. Watching him, Clayton enquired, 'Can you keep him alive until the judge gets here, Dr Petter?'

'He won't slip away yet, but' — the doctor held up the pinkish-coloured mixture in a glass — 'he'll need to have this before he can do any talking to the judge.'

Petters administered the potion, wiping the excess from the side of Bailey's mouth as Falk came back in with the judge. Looking down sympathetically at the burned man, Judge Landseer bent forward, asking, 'What do you have to tell me, son?'

As Bailey began to speak feebly, a shout came from outside.

'Roop Calmont!'

'That's Sheriff Decker,' a worried Clayton told his brother.

'He can wait,' Roop said.

'I know you're in there, Calmont,' Decker shouted again. 'I have here a warrant for your arrest.'

The shouting disturbed Bailey who convulsed twice, and stopped talking. Judge Landseer looked up anxiously to the doctor, who reached a hand to Bailey before saying, 'He's still alive, Judge Landseer, but that man shouting has to be stopped.'

'I'll stop him,' Roop said softly, and walked to the door.

'Roop,' Nancy called anxiously, following Roop out, her husband and Falk close behind her. Before closing the door, they heard the weak voice of Mitch Bailey recommence his testimony to Judge Landseer.

Pine Notch might have been unaware of their arrival, but now curious citizens lined the streets. Bennie Cault and his wife stood close enough to their store to be able to do business in the unlikely event of that requirement. Matt Brown was relating the past to a group of men interested only in the immediate present. Claude Sheen stood proudly in the doorway of his hotel, the pregnant Ellie clinging to his arm with both her hands. When Roop Calmont appeared she loosened her grip. It seemed she was about to rush towards him, but then, her face sad, she held on to her husband again.

Standing prominently in the centre of the street, his right hand held stiffly above his holstered gun, was Sheriff Derek Decker. His tense young body did a slight but discernible jerk as Roop stepped out of the doctor's house.

'You can play this how you like, Calmont,' Decker said. 'It makes no difference to me whether I lock you up or gun you down.'

Pat Shephard was standing off to the sheriff's right. Obviously fearful for

Decker, the deputy called to Roop, 'There ain't no need for gunplay here, Calmont.'

'You dealing yourself a hand in this, Shephard?' Roop calmly enquired.

'The way I see it this is between you and the law,' Pat Shephard answered, 'not between you and Decker.'

'Seems to me Decker doesn't see it that way,' Roop laconically remarked.

'You're danged right it isn't. You and me got a score to settle, Calmont,' Derek Decker said.

'Climb down from this, Sheriff,' Shephard advised. 'We'll take Calmont in and turn him over to the judge.'

Matt Brown had come closer to support Shephard, saying, 'Pat's right, son. Pine Notch came of age a long time ago. We don't want no killing on the streets these days.'

What both Brown and Shephard said had the opposite to the intended effect on Decker. Knowing that they were convinced he was going to die damaged his fragile pride further.

'Keep back, Pat,' he snarled. 'And you, old man. Come on Calmont: I'm waiting.'

'Do something, Falk,' Shephard appealed to the deputy US marshal.

'I can't,' Falk explained. 'There's no crime been committed.'

'I'm getting mighty impatient, Calmont,' Decker said.

Turning his head slightly, Roop looked at his brother. Then his eyes met Nancy's and held them for a moment. She put her hand to her mouth in fear as he broke the eye contact to walk out into the centre of the street.

The whole town went totally silent. Not even a horse dared move or a bird sing as Roop Calmont walked slowly towards Derek Decker. Folk knew that though they were in life they were truly in the midst of death as the Good Book said. Though hating what was about to happen, some macabre side of human nature meant that none of them, not even the women, wanted to miss it.

When it did happen it was with

eye-baffling speed. Most believed they heard only a single shot, and all they were definitely aware of was the sight of Sheriff Decker standing with a smoking gun in his hand. This wasn't the expected outcome, and all eyes turned to Roop Calmont.

The townsfolk gasped in unison as Roop's knees buckled and he sank to the ground like a man overcome by a sudden weariness. No one made a move, not even Derek Decker. Then a short, anguished scream split the air as Ellie Sheen, ungainly in her pregnancy, ran to drop down and lie across the body of Roop Calmont, hugging it as she sobbed loudly.

Further up the street, the shattered husband she had left behind, turned and walked back into the Peak View Hotel, head down and feet dragging. As the wailing of Ellie grew in volume, the mystified people of Pine Notch remained unmoving.

'I got him! I got Roop Calmont!' Derek Decker crowed as Susan Staker, smiling through tears she had been ready to shed, and could not now take back, ran to his side.

Giving the sheriff a contemptuous look, Pat Shephard walked over to look down at the dead Roop Calmont, a frown on his face. Sitting on his heels, Shephard moved the grieving Ellie's skirt a little to one side so as to take a closer look at the dead man.

Pat Shephard murmured to himself, 'Now why didn't Roop even go for his gun?'

Hearing the question, Nancy was the only one who knew the answer, the only one who would ever know. Weeping, she pressed herself against her husband.

'Hold me, Clayton,' Nancy pleaded. 'Hold me tightly.'

THE END

We do hope that you have enjoyed reading this large print book.

Did you know that all of our titles are available for purchase?

We publish a wide range of high quality large print books including:
Romances, Mysteries, Classics, General Fiction, Non Fiction and Westerns.

Special interest titles available in large print are:
The Little Oxford Dictionary Music Book, Song Book Hymn Book, Service Book

Also available from us courtesy of Oxford University Press:
Young Readers' Dictionary (large print edition) Young Readers' Thesaurus (large print edition)

For further information or a free brochure, please contact us at:
**Ulverscroft Large Print Books Ltd., The Green, Bradgate Road, Anstey, Leicester, LE7 7FU, England.
Tel:** (00 44) **0116 236 4325
Fax:** (00 44) **0116 234 0205**